The Wolves and the Lamb by William Makepeace Thackeray

The great author of Vanity Fair and The Luck Of Barry Lyndon was born in India in 1811.

At age 5 his father died and his mother sent him back to England. His education was of the best but he himself seemed unable to apply his talents to a rigorous work ethic.

However, once he harnessed his talents the works flowed in novels, articles, short stories, sketches and lectures.

Sadly, his personal life was rather more difficult. After a few years of marriage his wife began to suffer from depression and over the years became detached from reality. Thackeray himself suffered from ill health later in his life and the one pursuit that kept him moving forward was that of writing. In his life time, he was placed second only to Dickens. High praise indeed.

Index of Contents

THE WOLVES AND THE LAMB

DRAMATIS PERSONAE
MR. HORACE MILLIKEN, a Widower, a wealthy City Merchant.
GEORGE MILLIKEN, a Child, his Son.
CAPTAIN TOUCHIT, his Friend.
CLARENCE KICKLEBURY, brother to Milliken's late Wife.
JOHN HOWELL, M's Butler and confidential Servant.
CHARLES PAGE, Foot-boy.
BULKELEY, Lady Kicklebury's Servant.
MR. BONNINGTON.
Coachman, Cabman; a Bluecoat Boy, another Boy (Mrs. Prior's Sons).

LADY KICKLEBURY, Mother-in-law to Milliken.
MRS. BONNINGTON, Milliken's Mother (married again).
MRS. PRIOR.
MISS PRIOR, her Daughter, Governess to Milliken's Children.
ARABELLA MILLIKEN, a Child.
MARY BARLOW, School-room Maid.

A grown-up Girl and Child of Mrs. Prior's, Lady K.'s Maid, Cook.

ACT I

SCENE

Milliken's villa at Richmond; two drawing-rooms opening into one another. The late Mrs Milliken's portrait over the mantel-piece; bookcases, writing-tables, piano, newspapers, a handsomely furnished saloon. The back-room opens, with very large windows, on the lawn and pleasure-ground; gate, and wall—over which the heads of a cab and a carriage are seen, as persons arrive. Fruit, and a ladder on the walls. A door to the dining-room, another to the sleeping-apartments, &c.

JOHN
Everybody out; governor in the city; governess (heigh-ho!) walking in the Park with the children; ladyship gone out in the carriage. Let's sit down and have a look at the papers. Buttons fetch the Morning Post out of Lady Kicklebury's room. Where's the Daily News, sir?

PAGE
Think it's in Milliken's room.

JOHN
Milliken! you scoundrel! What do you mean by Milliken? Speak of your employer as your governor if you like; but not as simple Milliken. Confound your impudence! you'll be calling me Howell next.

PAGE
Well! I didn't know. YOU call him Milliken.

JOHN
Because I know him, because I'm intimate with him, because there's not a secret he has but I may have it for the asking; because the letters addressed to Horace Milliken, Esq., might as well be addressed John Howell, Esq., for I read 'em, I put 'em away and docket 'em, and remember 'em. I know his affairs better than he does: his income to a shilling, pay his tradesmen, wear his coats if I like. I may call Mr. Milliken what I please; but not YOU, you little scamp of a clod-hopping ploughboy. Know your station and do your business, or you don't wear THEM buttons long, I promise you.

[Exit **PAGE**.]

Let me go on with the paper [Reads]. How brilliant this writing is! Times, Chronicle, Daily News, they're all good, blest if they ain't. How much better the nine leaders in them three daily papers is, than nine speeches in the House of Commons! Take a very best speech in the 'Ouse now, and compare it with an article in The Times! I say, the newspaper has the best of it for philosophy, for wit, novelty, good sense too. And the party that writes the leading article is nobody, and the chap that speaks in the House of Commons is a hero. Lord, Lord, how the world is 'umbugged! Pop'lar representation! what IS pop'lar representation? Dammy, it's a farce. Hallo! this article is stole! I remember a passage in Montesquieu uncommonly like it.

[Goes and gets the book. As he is standing upon sofa to get it, and sitting down to read it, **MISS PRIOR** and the **CHILDREN** have come in at the garden. **CHILDREN** pass across stage. **MISS PRIOR** enters by open window, bringing flowers into the room.]

JOHN
It IS like it.

[He slaps the book, and seeing **MISS PRIOR** who enters, then jumps up from sofa, saying very respectfully,]

JOHN
I beg your pardon, Miss.

MISS PRIOR [Sarcastically.]
Do I disturb you, Howell?

JOHN
Disturb! I have no right to say—a servant has no right to be disturbed, but I hope I may be pardoned for venturing to look at a volume in the libery, Miss, just in reference to a newspaper harticle—that's all, Miss.

MISS PRIOR
You are very fortunate in finding anything to interest you in the paper, I'm sure.

JOHN
Perhaps, Miss, you are not accustomed to political discussion, and ignorant of—ah—I beg your pardon: a servant, I know, has no right to speak.

[Exit into dining-room, making a low bow.]

MISS PRIOR
The coolness of some people is really quite extraordinary! the airs they give themselves, the way in which they answer one, the books they read! Montesquieu: "Esprit des Lois!"

[Takes book up which J. has left on sofa.]

I believe the man has actually taken this from the shelf. I am sure Mr. Milliken, or her ladyship, never would. The other day "Helvetius" was found in Mr. Howell's pantry, forsooth! It is wonderful how he picked up French whilst we were abroad. "Esprit des Lois!" what is it? it must be dreadfully stupid. And as for reading "Helvetius" (who, I suppose, was a Roman general), I really can't understand how—Dear, dear! what airs these persons give themselves! What will come next? A footman—I beg Mr. Howell's pardon—a butler and confidential valet lolls on the drawing-room sofa, and reads Montesquieu! Impudence! And add to this, he follows me for the last two or three months with eyes that are quite horrid. What can the creature mean? But I forgot—I am only a governess. A governess is not a lady—a governess is but a servant—a governess is to work and walk all day with the children, dine in the school-room, and come to the drawing-room to play the man of the house to sleep. A governess is a domestic, only her place is not the servants' hall, and she is paid not quite so well as the butler who serves her her glass of wine. Odious! George! Arabella! there are those little wretches quarrelling again!

[Exit. **CHILDREN** are heard calling out, and seen quarrelling in garden.]

JOHN [Re-entering]
See where she moves! grace is in all her steps. 'Eaven in her high—no—a-heaven in her heye, in every gesture dignity and love—ah, I wish I could say it! I wish you may procure it, poor fool! She passes by me—she tr-r-amples on me. Here's the chair she sets in

[Kisses it.]

Here's the piano she plays on. Pretty keys, them fingers out-hivories you! When she plays on it, I stand and listen at the drawing-room door, and my heart thr-obs in time! Fool, fool, fool! why did you look on her, John Howell! why did you beat for her, busy heart! You were tranquil till you knew her! I thought I could have been a-happy with Mary till then. That girl's affection soothed me. Her conversation didn't amuse me much, her ideers ain't exactly elevated, but they are just and proper. Her attentions pleased me. She ever kep' the best cup of tea for me. She crisped my buttered toast, or mixed my quiet tumbler for me, as I sat of hevenings and read my newspaper in the kitching. She respected the sanctaty of my pantry. When I was a-studying there, she never interrupted me. She darned my stockings for me, she starched and folded my chokers, and she sowed on the habsent buttons of which time and chance had bereft my linning. She has a good heart, Mary has. I know she'd get up and black the boots for me of the coldest winter mornings. She did when we was in humbler life, she did.

[Enter **MARY**.

You have a good heart, Mary!

MARY
Have I, dear John? [Sadly.]

JOHN
Yes, child—yes. I think a better never beat in woman's bosom. You're good to everybody—good to your parents whom you send half your wages to: good to your employers whom you never robbed of a halfpenny.

MARY [Whimpering]
Yes, I did, John. I took the jelly when you were in bed with the influenza; and brought you the pork-wine negus.

JOHN
Port, not pork, child. Pork is the hanimal which Jews ab'or. Port is from Oporto in Portugal.

MARY [Still crying]
Yes, John; you know everything a'most, John.

JOHN
And you, poor child, but little! It's not heart you want, you little trump, it's education, Mary: it's information: it's head, head, head! You can't learn. You never can learn. Your ideers ain't no good. You

never can hinterchange em with mine. Conversation between us is impossible. It's not your fault. Some people are born clever; some are born tall, I ain't tall.

MARY
Ho! you're big enough for me, John.

[Offers to take his hand.]

JOHN
Let go my 'and—my a-hand, Mary! I say, some people are born with brains, and some with big figures. Look at that great ass, Bulkeley, Lady K.'s man—the besotted, stupid beast! He's as big as a life-guardsman, but he ain't no more education nor ideers than the ox he feeds on.

MARY
Law, John, whatever do you mean?

JOHN
Hm! you know not, little one! you never can know. Have YOU ever felt the pangs of imprisoned genius? have YOU ever felt what 'tis to be a slave?

MARY
Not in a free country, I should hope, John Howell—no such a thing. A place is a place, and I know mine, and am content with the spear of life in which it pleases heaven to place me, John: and I wish you were, and remembered what we learned from our parson when we went to school together in dear old Pigeoncot, John—when you used to help little Mary with her lessons, John, and fought Bob Brown, the big butcher's boy, because he was rude to me, John, and he gave you that black hi.

JOHN
Say eye, Mary, not heye [gently].

MARY
Eye; and I thought you never looked better in all your life than you did then: and we both took service at Squire Milliken's—me as dairy-girl, and you as knife-boy; and good masters have they been to us from our youth hup: both old Squire Milliken and Mr. Charles as is master now, and poor Mrs. as is dead, though she had her tantrums—and I thought we should save up and take the "Milliken Arms"—and now we have saved up—and now, now, now—oh, you are a stone, a stone, a stone! and I wish you were hung round my neck, and I were put down the well! There's the hup-stairs bell.

[She starts, changing her manner as she hears the bell, and exit.]

JOHN [Looking after her]
It's all true. Gospel-true. We were children in the same village—sat on the same form at school. And it was for her sake that Bob Brown the butcher's boy whopped me. A black eye! I'm not handsome. But if I were ugly, ugly as the Saracen's 'Ead, ugly as that beast Bulkeley, I know it would be all the same to Mary. SHE has never forgot the boy she loved, that brought birds'-nests for her, and spent his halfpenny on cherries, and bought a fairing with his first half-crown—a brooch it was, I remember, of two billing doves a-hopping on one twig, and brought it home for little yellow-haired, blue-eyed, red-cheeked

Mary. Lord, Lord! I don't like to think how I've kissed 'em, the pretty cheeks! they've got quite pale now with crying—and she has never once reproached me, not once, the trump, the little tr-rump!

Is it my fault [stamping] that Fate has separated us? Why did my young master take me up to Oxford, and give me the run of his libery and the society of the best scouts in the University? Why did he take me abroad? Why have I been to Italy, France, Jummany with him—their manners noted and their realms surveyed, by jingo! I've improved myself, and Mary has remained as you was. I try a conversation, and she can't respond. She's never got a word of poetry beyond Watt's Ims, and if I talk of Byron or Moore to her, I'm blest if she knows anything more about 'em than the cook, who is as hignorant as a pig, or that beast Bulkeley, Lady Kick's footman. Above all, why, why did I see the woman upon whom my wretched heart is fixed for ever, and who carries away my soul with her—prostrate, I say, prostrate, through the mud at the skirts of her gownd! Enslaver! why did I ever come near you? O enchantress Kelipso! how you have got hold of me! It was Fate, Fate, Fate. When Mrs. Milliken fell ill of scarlet fever at Naples, Milliken was away at Petersborough, Rooshia, looking after his property. Her foring woman fled. Me and the governess remained and nursed her and the children. We nursed the little ones out of the fever. We buried their mother. We brought the children home over Halp and Happenine. I nursed 'em all three. I tended 'em all three, the orphans, and the lovely gu-gu-governess. At Rome, where she took ill, I waited on her; as we went to Florence, had we been attacked by twenty thousand brigands, this little arm had courage for them all! And if I loved thee, Julia, was I wrong? and if I basked in thy beauty day and night, Julia, am I not a man? and if, before this Peri, this enchantress, this gazelle, I forgot poor little Mary Barlow, how could I help it? I say, how the doose could I help it?

[Enter **LADY KICKLEBURY, BULKELEY** following with parcels and a spaniel.

LADY KICKLEBURY
Are the children and the governess come home?

JOHN
Yes, my lady [in a perfectly altered tone].

LADY KICKLEBURY
Bulkeley, take those parcels to my sitting-room.

JOHN
Get up, old stoopid. Push along, old daddylonglegs [Aside to **BULKELEY**].

LADY KICKLEBURY
Does any one dine here to-day, Howell?

JOHN
Captain Touchit, my lady.

LADY KICKLEBURY
He's always dining here.

JOHN
My master's oldest friend.

LADY KICKLEBURY

Don't tell me. He comes from his club. He smells of smoke; he is a low, vulgar person. Send Pinhorn up to me when you go down stairs.

[Exit LADY **KICKLEBURY**.]

JOHN

I know. Send Pinhorn to me, means, Send my bonny brown hair, and send my beautiful complexion, and send my figure—and, O Lord! O Lord! what an old tigress that is! What an old Hector! How she do twist Milliken round her thumb! He's born to be bullied by women: and I remember him henpecked—let's see, ever since—ever since the time of that little gloveress at Woodstock, whose picter poor Mrs. M. made such a noise about when she found it in the lumber-room. Heh! HER picture will be going into the lumber-room some day. M. must marry to get rid of his mother-in-law and mother over him: no man can stand it, not M. himself, who's a Job of a man. Isn't he, look at him!

[As he has been speaking, the bell has rung, the **PAGE** has run to the garden-door, and **MILLIKEN** enters through the garden, laden with a hamper, band-box, and cricket-bat.]

MILLIKEN

Why was the carriage not sent for me, Howell? There was no cab at the station, and I have had to toil all the way up the hill with these confounded parcels of my lady's.

JOHN

I suppose the shower took off all the cabs, sir. When DID a man ever git a cab in a shower?—or a policeman at a pinch—or a friend when you wanted him—or anything at the right time, sir?

MILLIKEN

But, sir, why didn't the carriage come, I say?

JOHN

YOU know.

MILLIKEN

How do you mean I know? confound your impudence!

JOHN

Lady Kicklebury took it—your mother-in-law took it—went out a-visiting—Ham Common, Petersham, Twick'nam—doose knows where. She, and her footman, and her span'l dog.

MILLIKEN

Well, sir, suppose her ladyship DID take the carriage? Hasn't she a perfect right? And if the carriage was gone, I want to know, John, why the devil the pony-chaise wasn't sent with the groom? Am I to bring a bonnet-box and a hamper of fish in my own hands, I should like to know?

JOHN

Heh! [laughs.]

MILLIKEN

Why do you grin, you Cheshire cat?

JOHN
Your mother-in-law had the carriage; and your mother sent for the pony-chaise. Your Pa wanted to go and see the Wicar of Putney. Mr. Bonnington don't like walking when he can ride.

MILLIKEN
And why shouldn't Mr. Bonnington ride, sir, as long as there's a carriage in my stable? Mr. Bonnington has had the gout, sir! Mr. Bonnington is a clergyman, and married to my mother. He has EVERY title to my respect.

JOHN
And to your pony-chaise—yes, sir.

MILLIKEN
And to everything he likes in this house, sir.

JOHN
What a good fellow you are, sir! You'd give your head off your shoulders, that you would. Is the fish for dinner to-day? Band-box for my lady, I suppose, sir? [Looks in]—Turban, feathers, bugles, marabouts, spangles—doose knows what. Yes, it's for her ladyship. [To **PAGE**.] Charles, take this band-box to her ladyship's maid. [To his master.] What sauce would you like with the turbot? Lobster sauce or Hollandaise? Hollandaise is best—most wholesome for you. Anybody besides Captain Touchit coming to dinner?

MILLIKEN
No one that I know of.

JOHN
Very good. Bring up a bottle of the brown hock? He likes the brown hock, Touchit does.

[Exit **JOHN**.]

[Enter **CHILDREN**. They run to **MILLIKEN**.

BOTH
How d'you do, Papa! How do you do, Papa!

MILLIKEN
Kiss your old father, Arabella. Come here, George—What?

GEORGE
Don't care for kissing—kissing's for gals. Have you brought me that bat from London?

MILLIKEN
Yes. Here's the bat; and here's the ball—

[Takes one from pocket]

—and—

GEORGE
Where's the wickets, Papa. O-o-o—where's the wickets?

[Howls.]

MILLIKEN
My dear, darling boy! I left them at the office. What a silly papa I was to forget them! Parkins forgot them.

GEORGE
Then turn him away, I say! Turn him away!

[He stamps.]

MILLIKEN
What! an old, faithful clerk and servant of your father and grandfather for thirty years past? An old man, who loves us all, and has nothing but our pay to live on?

ARABELLA
Oh, you naughty boy!

GEORGE
I ain't a naughty boy.

ARABELLA
You are a naughty boy.

GEORGE
He! he! he! he!

[Grins at her.]

MILLIKEN
Hush, children! Here, Arabella darling, here is a book for you. Look—aren't they pretty pictures?

ARABELLA
Is it a story, Papa? I don't care for stories in general. I like something instructive and serious. Grandmamma Bonnington and grandpapa say—

GEORGE
He's NOT your grandpapa.

ARABELLA
He IS my grandpapa.

GEORGE
Oh, you great story! Look! look! there's a cab.

[Runs out. The head of a Hansom cab is seen over the garden-gate. Bell rings. **PAGE** comes. Altercation between **CABMAN** and **CAPTAIN TOUCHIT** appears to go on, during which]

MILLIKEN
Come and kiss your old father, Arabella. He's hungry for kisses.

ARABELLA
Don't. I want to go and look at the cab; and to tell Captain Touchit that he mustn't use naughty words.

[Runs towards garden. **PAGE** is seen carrying a carpet-bag.]

[Enter **TOUCHIT** through the open window smoking a cigar.

TOUCHIT
How d'ye do, Milliken? How are tallows, hey, my noble merchant? I have brought my bag, and intend to sleep—

GEORGE
I say, godpapa—

TOUCHIT
Well, godson!

GEORGE
Give us a cigar!

TOUCHIT
Oh, you enfant terrible!

MILLIKEN [Wheezily]
Ah—ahem—George Touchit! you wouldn't mind—a—smoking that cigar in the garden, would you? Ah—ah!

TOUCHIT
Hullo! What's in the wind now? You used to be a most inveterate smoker, Horace.

MILLIKEN
The fact is—my mother-in-law—Lady Kicklebury—doesn't like it, and while she's with us, you know—

TOUCHIT
Of course, of course—

[Throws away cigar].

I beg her ladyship's pardon. I remember when you were courting her daughter she used not to mind it.

MILLIKEN

Don't—don't allude to those times.

[He looks up at his wife's picture.]

GEORGE

My mamma was a Kicklebury. The Kickleburys are the oldest family in all the world. My name is George Kicklebury Milliken, of Pigeoncot, Hants; the Grove, Richmond, Surrey; and Portland Place, London, Esquire—my name is.

TOUCHIT

You have forgotten Billiter Street, hemp and tallow merchant.

GEORGE

Oh, bother! I don't care about that. I shall leave that when I'm a man: when I'm a man and come into my property.

MILLIKEN

You come into your property?

GEORGE

I shall, you know, when you're dead, Papa. I shall have this house, and Pigeoncot; and the house in town—no, I don't mind about the house in town—and I shan't let Bella live with me—no, I won't.

BELLA

No; I won't live with YOU. And I'LL have Pigeoncot.

GEORGE

You shan't have Pigeoncot. I'll have it: and the ponies: and I won't let you ride them—and the dogs, and you shan't have even a puppy to play with and the dairy and won't I have as much cream as I like—that's all!

TOUCHIT

What a darling boy! Your children are brought up beautifully, Milliken. It's quite delightful to see them together.

GEORGE

And I shall sink the name of Milliken, I shall.

MILLIKEN

Sink the name? why, George?

GEORGE

Because the Millikens are nobodies—grandmamma says they are nobodies. The Kickleburys are gentlemen, and came over with William the Conqueror.

BELLA

I know when that was. One thousand one hundred and one thousand one hundred and onety-one!

GEORGE
Bother when they came over! But I know this, when I come into the property I shall sink the name of Milliken.

MILLIKEN
So you are ashamed of your father's name, are you, George, my boy?

GEORGE
Ashamed! No, I ain't ashamed. Only Kicklebury is sweller. I know it is. Grandmamma says so.

BELLA
MY grandmamma does not say so. MY dear grandmamma says that family pride is sinful, and all belongs to this wicked world; and that in a very few years what our names are will not matter.

GEORGE
Yes, she says so because her father kept a shop; and so did Pa's father keep a sort of shop—only Pa's a gentleman now.

TOUCHIT
Darling child! How I wish I were married! If I had such a dear boy as you, George, do you know what I would give him?

GEORGE [Quite pleased]
What would you give him, god-papa?

TOUCHIT
I would give him as sound a flogging as ever boy had, my darling. I would whip this nonsense out of him. I would send him to school, where I would pray that he might be well thrashed: and if when he came home he was still ashamed of his father, I would put him apprentice to a chimney-sweep—that's what I would do.

GEORGE
I'm glad you're not my father, that's all.

BELLA
And I'M glad you're not my father, because you are a wicked man!

MILLIKEN
Arabella!

BELLA
Grandmamma says so. He is a worldly man, and the world is wicked. And he goes to the play: and he smokes, and he says—

TOUCHIT
Bella, what do I say?

BELLA

Oh, something dreadful! You know you do! I heard you say it to the cabman.

TOUCHIT

So I did, so I did! He asked me fifteen shillings from Piccadilly, and I told him to go to—to somebody whose name begins with a D.

CHILDREN

Here's another carriage passing.

BELLA

The Lady Rumble's carriage.

GEORGE

No, it ain't: it's Captain Boxer's carriage

[They run into the garden].

TOUCHIT

And this is the pass to which you have brought yourself, Horace Milliken! Why, in your wife's time, it was better than this, my poor fellow!

MILLIKEN

Don't speak of her in THAT way, George Touchit!

TOUCHIT

What have I said? I am only regretting her loss for our sake. She tyrannized over you; turned your friends out of doors; took your name out of your clubs; dragged you about from party to party, though you can no more dance than a bear, and from opera to opera, though you don't know "God Save the Queen" from "Rule Britannia." You don't, sir; you know you don't. But Arabella was better than her mother, who has taken possession of you since your widowhood.

MILLIKEN

My dear fellow! no, she hasn't. There's MY mother.

TOUCHIT

Yes, to be sure, there's Mrs. Bonnington, and they quarrel over you like the two ladies over the baby before King Solomon.

MILLIKEN

Play the satirist, my good friend! laugh at my weakness!

TOUCHIT

I know you to be as plucky a fellow as ever stepped, Milliken, when a man's in the case. I know you and I stood up to each other for an hour and a half at Westminster.

MILLIKEN

Thank you! We were both dragons of war! tremendous champions! Perhaps I am a little soft as regards women. I know my weakness well enough; but in my case what is my remedy? Put yourself in my position. Be a widower with two young children. What is more natural than that the mother of my poor wife should come and superintend my family? My own mother can't. She has a half-dozen of little half brothers and sisters, and a husband of her own to attend to. I dare say Mr. Bonnington and my mother will come to dinner to-day.

TOUCHIT
Of course they will, my poor old Milliken, you don't dare to dine without them.

MILLIKEN
Don't go on in that manner, George Touchit! Why should not my step-father and my mother dine with me? I can afford it. I am a domestic man and like to see my relations about me. I am in the city all day.

TOUCHIT
Luckily for you.

MILLIKEN
And my pleasure of an evening is to sit under my own vine and under my own fig-tree with my own olive-branches round about me; to sit by my fire with my children at my knees: to coze over a snug bottle of claret after dinner with a friend like you to share it; to see the young folks at the breakfast-table of a morning, and to kiss them and so off to business with a cheerful heart. This was my scheme in marrying, had it pleased heaven to prosper my plan. When I was a boy and came from school and college, I used to see Mr. Bonnington, my father-in-law, with HIS young ones clustering round about him, so happy to be with him! so eager to wait on him! all down on their little knees round my mother before breakfast or jumping up on his after dinner. It was who should reach his hat, and who should bring his coat, and who should fetch his umbrella, and who should get the last kiss.

TOUCHIT
What? didn't he kiss YOU? Oh, the hard-hearted old ogre!

MILLIKEN
DON'T, Touchit! Don't laugh at Mr. Bonnington! he is as good a fellow as ever breathed. Between you and me, as my half brothers and sisters increased and multiplied year after year, I used to feel rather lonely, rather bowled out, you understand. But I saw them so happy that I longed to have a home of my own. When my mother proposed Arabella for me (for she and Lady Kicklebury were immense friends at one time), I was glad enough to give up clubs and bachelorhood, and to settle down as a married man. My mother acted for the best. My poor wife's character, my mother used to say, changed after marriage. I was not as happy as I hoped to be; but I tried for it. George, I am not so comfortable now as I might be. A house without a mistress, with two mothers-in-law reigning over it—one worldly and aristocratic, another what you call serious, though she don't mind a rubber of whist; I give you my honor my mother plays a game at whist, and an uncommonly good game too—each woman dragging over a child to her side: of course such a family cannot be comfortable.

[Bell rings.]

There's the first dinner-bell. Go and dress, for heaven's sake.

TOUCHIT
Why dress? There is no company!

MILLIKEN
Why? ah! her ladyship likes it, you see. And it costs nothing to humor her. Quick, for she don't like to be kept waiting.

TOUCHIT
Horace Milliken! what a pity it is the law declares a widower shall not marry his wife's mother! She would marry you else,—she would, on my word.

[Enter **JOHN**.

JOHN
I have took the Captain's things in the blue room, sir.

[Exeunt **GENTLEMEN**, **JOHN** arranges tables, &c.]

Ha! Mrs. Prior! I ain't partial to Mrs. Prior. I think she's an artful old dodger, Mrs. Prior. I think there's mystery in her unfathomable pockets, and schemes in the folds of her umbrella. But—but she's Julia's mother, and for the beloved one's sake I am civil to her.

MRS PRIOR
Thank you Charles [To the **PAGE**, who has been seen to let her in at the garden-gate], I am so much obliged to you! Good afternoon, Mr. Howell. Is my daughter—are the darling children well? Oh, I am quite tired and weary! Three horrid omnibuses were full, and I have had to walk the whole weary long way. Ah, times are changed with me, Mr. Howell. Once when I was young and strong, I had my husband's carriage to ride in.

JOHN [Aside]
His carriage! his coal-wagon! I know well enough who old Prior was. A merchant? yes, a pretty merchant! kep' a lodging-house, share in a barge, touting for orders, and at last a snug little place in the Gazette.

MRS PRIOR
How is your cough, Mr. Howell? I have brought you some lozenges for it—

[Takes numberless articles from her pocket]

—and if you would take them of a night and morning—oh, indeed, you would get better! The late Sir Henry Halford recommended them to Mr. Prior. He was his late Majesty's physician and ours. You know we have seen happier times, Mr. Howell. Oh, I am quite tired and faint.

JOHN
Will you take anything before the school-room tea, ma'am? You will stop to tea, I hope, with Miss Prior, and our young folks?

MRS PRIOR

Thank you: a little glass of wine when one is so faint—a little crumb of biscuit when one is so old and tired! I have not been accustomed to want, you know; and in my poor dear Mr. Prior's time—

JOHN
I'll fetch some wine, ma'am.

[Exit to the dining-room.]

MRS PRIOR
Bless the man, how abrupt he is in his manner! He quite shocks a poor lady who has been used to better days. What's here? Invitations—ho! Bills for Lady Kicklebury! THEY are not paid. Where is Mr. M. going to dine, I wonder? Captain and Mrs. Hopkinson, Sir John and Lady Tomkinson, request the pleasure. Request the pleasure! Of course they do. They are always asking Mr. M. to dinner. They have daughters to marry, and Mr. M. is a widower with three thousand a year, every shilling of it. I must tell Lady Kicklebury. He must never go to these places—never, never—mustn't be allowed.

[While talking, she opens all the letters on the table, rummages the portfolio and writing-box, looks at cards on mantelpiece, work in work-basket, tries tea-box, and shows the greatest activity and curiosity.]

[Re-enter **JOHN**, bearing a tray with cakes, a decanter, &c.

Thank you, thank you, Mr. Howell! Oh, oh, dear me, not so much as that! Half a glass, and ONE biscuit, please. What elegant sherry!

[Sips a little, and puts down glass on tray].

Do you know, I remember in better days, Mr. Howell, when my poor dear husband—

JOHN
Beg your pardon. There's Milliken's bell, going like mad.

[Exit **JOHN**.]

MRS PRIOR
What an abrupt person! Oh, but it's comfortable, this wine is! And—and I think how my poor Charlotte would like a little—she so weak, and ordered wine by the medical man! And when dear Adolphus comes home from Christ's Hospital, quite tired, poor boy, and hungry, wouldn't a bit of nice cake do him good! Adolphus is so fond of plum-cake, the darling child! And so is Frederick, little saucy rogue; and I'll give them MY piece, and keep my glass of wine for my dear delicate angel Shatty!

[Takes bottle and paper out of her pocket, cuts off a great slice of cake, and pours wine from wine-glass and decanter into bottle.]

[Enter **PAGE**.

PAGE
Master George and Miss Bella is going to have their teas down here with Miss Prior, Mrs. Prior, and she's up in the school-room, and my lady says you may stay to tea.

MRS PRIOR

Thank you, Charles! How tall you grow! Those trousers would fit my darling Frederick to a nicety. Thank you, Charles. I know the way to the nursery.

[Exit **MRS PRIOR**]

PAGE

Know the way! I believe she DO know the way. Been a having cake and wine. Howell always gives her cake and wine—jolly cake, ain't it! and wine, oh, my!

[Re-enter **JOHN**.

JOHN

You young gormandizing cormorant! What! five meals a day ain't enough for you! What? beer ain't good enough for you, hey?

[Pulls **BOY'S** ears.]

PAGE [Crying]

Oh, oh, do-o-n't, Mr. Howell. I only took half a glass, upon my honor.

JOHN

Your a-honor, you lying young vagabond! I wonder the ground don't open and swallow you. Half a glass! [Holds up decanter.]

You've took half a bottle, you young Ananias! Mark this, sir! When I was a boy, a boy on my promotion, a child kindly took in from charity-school, a horphan in buttons like you, I never lied; no, nor never stole, and you've done both, you little scoundrel. Don't tell ME, sir! there's plums on your coat, crumbs on your cheek, and you smell sherry, sir! I ain't time to whop you now, but come to my pantry to-night after you've took the tray down. Come without your jacket on, sir, and then I'll teach you what it is to lie and steal. There's the outer bell. Scud, you vagabond!

[Enter **LADY KICKLEBURY**.

LADY KICKLEBURY

What was that noise, pray?

JOHN

A difference between me and young Page, my lady. I was instructing him to keep his hands from picking and stealing. I was learning him his lesson, my lady, and he was a-crying it out.

LADY KICKLEBURY

It seems to me you are most unkind to that boy, Howell. He is my boy, sir. He comes from my estate. I will not have him ill-used. I think you presume on your long services. I shall speak to my son-in-law about you. ["Yes, my lady; no, my lady; very good, my lady." **JOHN** has answered each sentence as she is speaking, and exit gravely bowing.] That man must quit the house. Horace says he can't do without him, but he must do without him. My poor dear Arabella was fond of him, but he presumes on that defunct angel's partiality. Horace says this person keeps all his accounts, sorts all his letters, manages all his affairs, may be trusted with untold gold, and rescued little George out of the fire. Now I have come to live with my son-in-law, I will keep his accounts, sort his letters, and take charge of his money: and if little Georgy gets into the grate, I will take him out of the fire. What is here? Invitation from Captain and Mrs. Hopkinson. Invitation from Sir John and Lady Tomkinson, who don't even ask me! Monstrous! he never shall go—he shall not go!

[**MRS. PRIOR** has re-entered, she drops a very low curtsy to **LADY KICKLEBURY**, as the latter, perceiving her, lays the cards down.]

MRS PRIOR

Ah, dear madam! how kind your ladyship's message was to the poor lonely widow woman! Oh, how thoughtful it was of your ladyship to ask me to stay to tea!

LADY KICKLEBURY

With your daughter and the children? Indeed, my good Mrs. Prior, you are very welcome!

MRS PRIOR

Ah! but isn't it a cause of thankfulness to be MADE welcome? Oughtn't I to be grateful for these blessings?—yes, I say BLESSINGS. And I am—I am, Lady Kicklebury—to the mother—of—that angel who is gone—

[Points to the picture].

It was your sainted daughter left us—left my child to the care of Mr. Milliken, and—and you, who are now his guardian angel I may say. You ARE, Lady Kicklebury—you are. I say to my girl, Julia, Lady Kicklebury is Mr. Milliken's guardian angel, is YOUR guardian angel—for without you could she keep her place as governess to these darling children? It would tear her heart in two to leave them, and yet she would be forced to do so. You know that some one—shall I hesitate to say whom I MEAN—that Mr. Milliken's mother, excellent lady though she is, does not love my child because YOU love her. You DO love her, Lady Kicklebury, and oh! a mother's fond heart pays you back! But for you, my poor Julia must go—go, and leave the children whom a dying angel confided to her!

LADY KICKLEBURY

Go! no, never! not whilst I am in this house, Mrs. Prior. Your daughter is a well-behaved young woman: you have confided to me her long engagement to Lieutenant—Lieutenant What-d'you-call'im, in the Indian service. She has been very, very good to my grandchildren—she brought them over from Naples when my—my angel of an Arabella died there, and I will protect Miss Prior.

MRS PRIOR

Bless you, bless you, noble, admirable woman! Don't take it away! I must, I WILL kiss your dear, generous hand! Take a mother's, a widow's blessings, Lady Kicklebury—the blessings of one who has known misfortune and seen better days, and thanks heaven!—yes, heaven!—for the protectors she has found!

LADY KICKLEBURY

You said—you had—several children, I think, my good Mrs. Prior?

MRS PRIOR
Three boys—one, my eldest blessing, is in a wine-merchant's office—ah, if Mr. Milliken WOULD but give him an order! an order from THIS house! an order from Lady Kicklebury's son-in-law!—

LADY KICKLEBURY
It shall be done, my good Prior—we will see.

MRS PRIOR
Another, Adolphus, dear fellow! is in Christ's Hospital. It was dear, good Mr. Milliken's nomination. Frederick is at Merchant Taylor's: my darling Julia pays his schooling. Besides, I have two girls—Amelia, quite a little toddles, just the size, though not so beautiful—but in a mother's eyes all children are lovely, dear Lady Kicklebury—just the size of your dear granddaughter, whose clothes would fit her, I am sure. And my second, Charlotte, a girl as tall as your ladyship, though not with so fine a figure. "Ah, no, Shatty!" I say to her, "you are as tall as our dear patroness, Lady Kicklebury, whom you long so to see; but you have not got her ladyship's carriage and figure, child." Five children have I, left fatherless and penniless by my poor dear husband—but heaven takes care of the widow and orphan, madam—and heaven's BEST CREATURES feed them!—YOU know whom I mean.

LADY KICKLEBURY
Should you not like, would you object to take—a frock or two of little Arabella's to your child? and if Pinhorn, my maid, will let me, Mrs. Prior, I will see if I cannot find something against winter for your second daughter, as you say we are of a size.

MRS PRIOR
The widow's and orphans' blessings upon you! I said my Charlotte was as tall, but I never said she had such a figure as yours—who has?

CHARLES announces—

CHARLES
Mrs. Bonnington!

[Enter **MRS BONNINGTON**.]

MRS BONNINGTON
How do you do, Lady Kicklebury?

LADY KICKLEBURY
My dear Mrs. Bonnington! and you come to dinner of course?

MRS BONNINGTON
To dine with my own son, I may take the liberty. How are my grandchildren? my darling little Emily, is she well, Mrs. Prior?

LADY KICKLEBURY [Aside]
Emily? why does she not call the child by her blessed mother's name of Arabella? [To **MRS BONNINGTON**] ARABELLA is quite well, Mrs. Bonnington. Mr. Squillings said it was nothing; only her

grandmamma Bonnington spoiling her, as usual. Mr. Bonnington and all your numerous young folk are well, I hope?

MRS BONNINGTON

My family are all in perfect health, I thank you. Is Horace come home from the city?

LADY KICKLEBURY

Goodness! there's the dinner-bell,—I must run to dress.

MRS PRIOR

Shall I come with you, dear Lady Kicklebury?

LADY KICKLEBURY

Not for worlds, my good Mrs. Prior.

[Exit **LADY KICKLEBURY**.]

MRS PRIOR

How do you do, my DEAR madam? Is dear Mr. Bonnington QUITE well? What a sweet, sweet sermon he gave us last Sunday. I often say to my girl, I must not go to hear Mr. Bonnington, I really must not, he makes me cry so. Oh! he is a great and gifted man, and shall I not have one glimpse of him?

MRS BONNINGTON

Saturday evening, my good Mrs. Prior. Don't you know that my husband never goes out on Saturday, having his sermon to compose?

MRS PRIOR

Oh, those dear, dear sermons! Do you know, madam, that my little Adolphus, for whom your son's bounty procured his place at Christ's Hospital, was very much touched indeed, the dear child, with Mr. Bonnington's discourse last Sunday three weeks, and refused to play marbles afterwards at school? The wicked, naughty boys beat the poor child; but Adolphus has his consolation! Is Master Edward well, ma'am, and Master Robert, and Master Frederick, and dear little funny Master William?

MRS BONNINGTON

Thank you, Mrs. Prior; you have a good heart, indeed!

MRS PRIOR

Ah, what blessings those dears are to you! I wish your dearest little GRANDSON—

MRS BONNINGTON

The little naughty wretch! Do you know, Mrs. Prior, my grandson, George Milliken, spilt the ink over my dear husband's bands, which he keeps in his great dictionary; and fought with my child, Frederick, who is three years older than George—actually beat his own uncle!

MRS PRIOR

Gracious mercy! Master Frederick was not hurt, I hope?

MRS BONNINGTON

No; he cried a great deal; and then Robert came up, and that graceless little George took a stick; and then my husband came out, and do you know George Milliken actually kicked Mr. Bonnington on his shins, and butted him like a little naughty ram?

MRS PRIOR

Mercy! mercy! what a little rebel! He is spoiled, dear madam, and you know by WHOM.

MRS BONNINGTON

By his grandmamma Kicklebury. I know it. I want my son to whip that child, but he refuses. He will come to no good; that child.

MRS PRIOR

Ah, madam, don't say so! Let us hope for the best. Master George's high temper will subside when certain persons who pet him are gone away.

MRS BONNINGTON

Gone away! they never will go away! No, mark my words, Mrs. Prior, that woman will never go away. She has made the house her own: she commands everything and everybody in it. She has driven me—me—Mr. Milliken's own mother—almost out of it. She has so annoyed my dear husband, that Mr. Bonnington will scarcely come here. Is she not always sneering at private tutors, because Mr. Bonnington was my son's private tutor, and greatly valued by the late Mr. Milliken? Is she not making constant allusions to old women marrying young men, because Mr. Bonnington happens to be younger than me? I have no words to express my indignation respecting Lady Kicklebury. She never pays any one, and runs up debts in the whole town. Her man Bulkeley's conduct in the neighborhood is quite—quite—

MRS PRIOR

Gracious goodness, ma'am, you don't say so! And then what an appetite the gormandizing monster has! Mary tells me that what he eats in the servants' hall is something perfectly frightful.

MRS BONNINGTON

Everybody feeds on my poor son! You are looking at my cap, Mrs. Prior?

[During this time **MRS PRIOR** has been peering into a parcel which **MRS BONNINGTON** brought in her hand.]

I brought it with me across the Park. I could not walk through the Park in my cap. Isn't it a pretty ribbon, Mrs. Prior?

MRS PRIOR

Beautiful! beautiful? How blue becomes you! Who would think you were the mother of Mr. Milliken and seven other darling children? You can afford what Lady Kicklebury cannot.

MRS BONNINGTON

And what is that, Prior? A poor clergyman's wife, with a large family, cannot afford much.

MRS PRIOR

He! he! You can afford to be seen as you are, which Lady K. cannot. Did you not remark how afraid she seemed lest I should enter her dressing-room? Only Pinhorn, her maid, goes there, to arrange the roses, and the lilies, and the figure—he! he! Oh, what a sweet, sweet cap-ribbon! When you have worn it, and are tired of it, you will give it me, won't you? It will be good enough for poor old Martha Prior!

MRS BONNINGTON
Do you really like it? Call at Greenwood Place, Mrs. Prior, the next time you pay Richmond a visit, and bring your little girl with you, and we will see.

MRS PRIOR
Oh, thank you! thank you! Nay, don't be offended! I must! I must!

[Kisses **MRS BONNINGTON**.]

MRS BONNINGTON
There, there! We must not stay chattering! The bell has rung. I must go and put the cap on, Mrs. Prior.

MRS PRIOR
And I may come too? YOU are not afraid of my seeing your hair, dear Mrs. Bonnington! Mr. Bonnington too young for YOU! Why, you don't look twenty!

MRS BONNINGTON
Oh, Mrs. Prior!

MRS PRIOR
Well, five-and-twenty, upon my word—not more than five-and-twenty—and that is the very prime of life.

[Exeunt **MRS BONNINGTON** and **MRS PRIOR**, hand in hand. As **CAPTAIN TOUCHIT** enters, dressed for dinner, he bows and passes on.]

TOUCHIT
So, we are to wear our white cravats, and our varnished boots, and dine in ceremony. What is the use of a man being a widower, if he can't dine in his shooting-jacket? Poor Mill! He has the slavery now without the wife.

[He speaks sarcastically to the picture.]

Well, well! Mrs. Milliken! YOU, at any rate, are gone; and with the utmost respect for you, I like your picture even better than the original. Miss Prior!

[Enter **MISS PRIOR**.

MISS PRIOR
I beg pardon. I thought you were gone to dinner. I heard the second bell some time since.

[She is drawing back.]

TOUCHIT
Stop! I say, Julia!

[She returns, he looks at her, takes her hand.]

Why do you dress yourself in this odd poky way? You used to be a very smartly dressed girl. Why do you hide your hair, and wear such a dowdy, high gown, Julia?

JULIA
You mustn't call me Julia, Captain Touchit.

TOUCHIT
Why? when I lived in your mother's lodging, I called you Julia. When you brought up the tea, you didn't mind being called Julia. When we used to go to the play with the tickets the Editor gave us, who lived on the second floor—

JULIA
The wretch!—don't speak of him!

TOUCHIT
Ah! I am afraid he was a sad deceiver, that Editor. He was a very clever fellow. What droll songs he used to sing! What a heap of play-tickets, diorama-tickets, concert-tickets, he used to give you! Did he touch your heart, Julia?

JULIA
Fiddlededee! No man ever touched my heart, Captain Touchit.

TOUCHIT
What! not even Tom Flight, who had the second floor after the Editor left it—and who cried so bitterly at the idea of going out to India without you? You had a tendre for him—a little passion—you know you had. Why, even the ladies here know it. Mrs. Bonnington told me that you were waiting for a sweetheart in India to whom you were engaged; and Lady Kicklebury thinks you are dying in love for the absent swain.

JULIA
I hope—I hope—you did not contradict them, Captain Touchit.

TOUCHIT
Why not, my dear?

JULIA
May I be frank with you? You were a kind, very kind friend to us—to me, in my youth.

TOUCHIT
I paid my lodgings regularly, and my bills without asking questions. I never weighed the tea in the caddy, or counted the lumps of sugar, or heeded the rapid consumption of my liqueur—

JULIA
Hush, hush! I know they were taken. I know you were very good to us. You helped my poor papa out of many a difficulty.

TOUCHIT [Aside]

Tipsy old coal-merchant! I did, and he helped himself too.

JULIA

And you were always our best friend, Captain Touchit. When our misfortunes came, you got me this situation with Mrs. Milliken—and, and—don't you see?—

TOUCHIT

Well—what?

JULIA [Laughing]

I think it is best, under the circumstances, that the ladies here should suppose I am engaged to be married—or or, they might be—might be jealous, you understand. Women are sometimes jealous of others,—especially mothers and mothers-in-law.

TOUCHIT

Oh, you arch schemer! And it is for that you cover up that beautiful hair of yours, and wear that demure cap?

JULIA [Slyly]

I am subject to rheumatism in the head, Captain Touchit.

TOUCHIT

It is for that you put on the spectacles, and make yourself look a hundred years old?

JULIA

My eyes are weak, Captain Touchit.

TOUCHIT

Weak with weeping for Tom Flight. You hypocrite! Show me your eyes!

MISS PRIOR

Nonsense!

TOUCHIT

Show me your eyes, I say, or I'll tell about Tom Flight and that he has been married at Madras these two years.

MISS PRIOR

Oh, you horrid man!

[Takes glasses off.]

There.

TOUCHIT

Translucent orbs! beams of flashing light! lovely lashes veiling celestial brightness! No, they haven't cried much for Tom Flight, that faithless captain! nor for Lawrence O'Reilly, that killing Editor. It is lucky you keep the glasses on them, or they would transfix Horace Milliken, my friend the widower here. DO you always wear them when you are alone with him?

MISS PRIOR

I never AM alone with him. Bless me! If Lady Kicklebury thought my eyes were—well, well—you know what I mean,—if she thought her son-in-law looked at me, I should be turned out of doors the next day, I am sure I should. And then, poor Mr. Milliken! he never looks at ME—heaven help him! Why, he can't see me for her ladyship's nose and awful caps and ribbons! He sits and looks at the portrait yonder, and sighs so. He thinks that he is lost in grief for his wife at this very moment.

TOUCHIT

What a woman that was—eh, Julia—that departed angel! What a temper she had before her departure!

MISS PRIOR

But the wind was tempered to the lamb. If she was angry—the lamb was so very lamblike, and meek, and fleecy.

TOUCHIT

And what a desperate flirt the departed angel was! I knew half a dozen fellows, before her marriage, whom she threw over, because Milliken was so rich.

MISS PRIOR

She was consistent at least, and did not change after marriage, as some ladies do; but flirted, as you call it, just as much as before. At Paris, young Mr. Verney, the attache, was never out of the house: at Rome, Mr. Beard, the artist, was always drawing pictures of her: at Naples, when poor Mr. M. went away to look after his affairs at St. Petersburg, little Count Posilippo was for ever coming to learn English and practise duets. She scarcely ever saw the poor children—

[Changing her manner as **LADY KICKLEBURY** enters]

Hush—my lady!

TOUCHIT

You may well say, "poor children," deprived of such a woman! Miss Prior, whom I knew in very early days—as your ladyship knows—was speaking—was speaking of the loss our poor friend sustained.

LADY KICKLEBURY

Ah, sir, what a loss!

[Looking at the picture.]

TOUCHIT

What a woman she was—what a superior creature!

LADY KICKLEBURY

A creature—an angel!

TOUCHIT

Mercy upon us! how she and my lady used to quarrel! [Aside.] What a temper!

LADY KICKLEBURY

Hm—oh, yes—what a temper [Rather doubtfully at first].

TOUCHIT

What a loss to Milliken and the darling children!

MISS PRIOR

Luckily they have YOU with them madam.

LADY KICKLEBURY

And I will stay with them, Miss Prior; I will stay with them! I will never part from Horace, I am determined.

MISS PRIOR

Ah! I am very glad you stay, for if I had not YOU for a protector, I think you know I must go, Lady Kicklebury. I think you know there are those who would forget my attachment to these darling children, my services to—to her—and dismiss the poor governess. But while you stay I can stay, dear Lady Kicklebury! With you to defend me from jealousy I need not QUITE be afraid.

LADY KICKLEBURY

Of Mrs. Bonnington? Of Mr. Milliken's mother; of the parson's wife who writes out his stupid sermons, and has half a dozen children of her own? I should think NOT indeed! I am the natural protector of these children. I am their mother. I have no husband! You STAY in this house, Miss Prior. You are a faithful, attached creature—though you were sent in by somebody I don't like very much.

[Pointing to **TOUCHIT**, who went off laughing when **JULIA** began her speech, and is now looking at prints, &c., in next room].

MISS PRIOR

Captain Touchit may not be in all things what one could wish. But his kindness has formed the happiness of my life in making me acquainted with YOU, ma'am: and I am sure you would not have me be ungrateful to him.

LADY KICKLEBURY

A most highly principled young woman.

[Goes out in garden and walks up and down with **CAPTAIN TOUCHIT**.]

[Enter **MRS BONNINGTON**.

MISS PRIOR

Oh, how glad I am you are come, Mrs. Bonnington. Have you brought me that pretty hymn you promised me? You always keep your promises, even to poor governesses. I read dear Mr. Bonnington's sermon! It was so interesting that I really could not think of going to sleep until I had read it all through;

it was delightful, but oh! it's still better when he preaches it! I hope I did not do wrong in copying a part of it? I wish to impress it on the children. There are some worldly influences at work with them, dear madam—

[Looking at **LADY KICKLEBURY** in the garden]

—which I do my feeble effort to—to modify. I wish YOU could come oftener.

MRS BONNINGTON
I will try, my dear—I will try. Emily has sweet dispositions.

MISS PRIOR
Ah, she takes after her grandmamma Bonnington!

MRS BONNINGTON
But George was sadly fractious just now in the school-room because I tried him with a tract.

MISS PRIOR
Let us hope for better times! Do be with your children, dear Mrs. Bonnington, as constantly as ever you can, for MY sake as well as theirs! I want protection and advice as well as they do. The GOVERNESS, dear lady, looks up to you as well as the pupils; SHE wants the teaching which you and dear Mr. Bonnington can give her! Ah, why could not Mr. and Mrs. Bonnington come and live here, I often think? The children would have companions in their dear young uncles and aunts; so pleasant it would be. The house is quite large enough; that is, if her ladyship did not occupy the three south rooms in the left wing. Ah, why, WHY couldn't you come?

MRS BONNINGTON
You are a kind, affectionate creature, Miss Prior. I do not very much like the gentleman who recommended you to Arabella, you know. But I do think he sent my son a good governess for his children.

[**TWO LADIES** walk up and down in front garden.

[**TOUCHIT** enters.]

TOUCHIT
Miss Julia Prior, you are a wonder! I watch you with respect and surprise.

MISS PRIOR
Me! what have I done? a poor friendless governess—respect ME?

TOUCHIT
I have a mind to tell those two ladies what I think of Miss Julia Prior. If they knew you as I know you, O Julia Prior, what a short reign yours would be!

MISS PRIOR
I have to manage them a little. Each separately it is not so difficult. But when they are together, oh, it is very hard sometimes.

[Enter **MILLIKEN** dressed, shakes hands with **MISS PRIOR.**]

MILLIKEN
Miss Prior! are you well? Have the children been good? and learned all their lessons?

MISS PRIOR
The children are pretty good, sir.

MILLIKEN
Well, that's a great deal as times go. Do not bother them with too much learning, Miss Prior. Let them have an easy life. Time enough for trouble when age comes.

[Enter **JOHN.**

JOHN
Dinner, sir.

[And exit.]

MILLIKEN
Dinner, ladies. My Lady Kicklebury?

[Gives arm to **LADY KICKLEBURY**].

LADY KICKLEBURY
My dear Horace, you SHOULDN'T shake hands with Miss Prior. You should keep people of that class at a distance, my dear creature.

[They go in to dinner, **CAPTAIN TOUCHIT** following with **MRS BONNINGTON**. As they go out, enter **MARY** with children's tea-tray, &c., children following, and after them **MRS PRIOR**. **MARY** gives her tea.]

MRS PRIOR
Thank you, Mary! You are so very kind! Oh, what delicious tea!

GEORGE
I say, Mrs. Prior, I dare say you would like to dine best, wouldn't you?

MRS PRIOR
Bless you, my darling love, I had my dinner at one o'clock with my children at home.

GEORGE
So had we: but we go in to dessert very often; and then don't we have cakes and oranges and candied-peel and macaroons and things! We are not to go in to-day; because Bella ate so many strawberries she made herself ill.

BELLA
So did you.

GEORGE

I'm a man, and men eat more than women, twice as much as women. When I'm a man I'll eat as much cake as ever I like. I say, Mary, give us the marmalade.

MRS PRIOR

Oh, what nice marmalade! I know of some poor children—

MISS PRIOR

Mamma! don't, mamma [In an imploring tone].

MRS PRIOR

I know of two poor children at home, who have very seldom nice marmalade and cake, young people.

GEORGE

You mean Adolphus and Frederick and Amelia, your children. Well, they shall have marmalade and cake.

BELLA

Oh, yes! I'll give them mine.

MRS PRIOR

Darling, dearest child!

GEORGE [His mouth full]

I won't give 'em mine: but they can have another pot, you know. You have always got a basket with you, Mrs. Prior. I know you have. You had it that day you took the cold fowl.

MRS PRIOR

For the poor blind black man! oh, how thankful he was!

GEORGE

I don't know whether it was for a black man. Mary, get us another pot of marmalade.

MARY

I don't know, Master George.

GEORGE

I WILL have another pot of marmalade. If you don't, I'll—I'll smash everything—I will.

BELLA

Oh, you naughty, rude boy!

GEORGE

Hold YOUR tongue! I WILL have it. Mary shall go and get it.

MRS PRIOR

Do humor him, Mary; and I'm sure my poor children at home will be the better for it.

GEORGE

There's your basket! now put this cake in, and this pat of butter, and this sugar. Hurray, hurray! Oh, what jolly fun! Tell Adolphus and Amelia I sent it to them—tell 'em they shall never want for anything as long as George Kicklebury Milliken, Esq., can give it 'em. Did Adolphus like my gray coat that I didn't want?

MISS PRIOR

You did not give him your new gray coat?

GEORGE

Don't you speak to me; I'm going to school—I'm not going to have no more governesses soon.

MRS PRIOR

Oh, my dear Master George, what a nice coat it is, and how well my poor boy looked in it!

MISS PRIOR

Don't, mamma! I pray and entreat you not to take the things!

[Enter **JOHN** from dining-room with a tray.

JOHN

Some cream, some jelly, a little champagne, Miss Prior; I thought you might like some.

GEORGE

Oh, jolly! give us hold of the jelly! give us a glass of champagne.

JOHN

I will not give you any.

GEORGE

I'll smash every glass in the room if you don't; I'll cut my fingers; I'll poison myself—there! I'll eat all this sealing-wax if you don't, and it's rank poison, you know it is.

MRS PRIOR

My dear Master George!

[Exit **JOHN**.]

GEORGE

Ha, ha! I knew you'd give it me; another boy taught me that.

BELLA

And a very naughty, rude boy.

GEORGE

He, he, he! hold your tongue Miss! And said he always got wine so; and so I used to do it to my poor mamma, Mrs. Prior. Usedn't to like mamma much.

BELLA

Oh, you wicked boy!

GEORGE

She usedn't to see us much. She used to say I tried her nerves: what's nerves, Mrs. Prior? Give us some more champagne! Will have it. Ha, ha, ha! ain't it jolly? Now I'll go out and have a run in the garden.

[Runs into garden].

MRS PRIOR

And you, my dear?

BELLA

I shall go and resume the perusal of the "Pilgrim's Progress," which my grandpapa, Mr. Bonnington, sent me.

[Exit **ARABELLA**.]

MISS PRIOR

How those children are spoilt! Goodness; what can I do? If I correct one, he flies to grandmamma Kicklebury; if I speak to another, she appeals to grandmamma Bonnington. When I was alone with them, I had them in something like order. Now, between the one grandmother and the other, the children are going to ruin, and so would the house too, but that Howell—that odd, rude, but honest and intelligent creature, I must say—keeps it up. It is wonderful how a person in his rank of life should have instructed himself so. He really knows—I really think he knows more than I do myself.

MRS PRIOR

Julia dear!

MISS PRIOR

What is it, mamma?

MRS PRIOR

Your little sister wants some underclothing sadly, Julia dear, and poor Adolphus's shoes are quite worn out.

MISS PRIOR

I thought so; I have given you all I could, mamma.

MRS PRIOR

Yes, my love! you are a good love, and generous, heaven knows, to your poor old mother who has seen better days. If we had not wanted, would I have ever allowed you to be a governess—a poor degraded governess? If that brute O'Reilly who lived on our second floor had not behaved so shamefully wicked to you, and married Miss Flack, the singer, might you not have been Editress of the Champion of Liberty at this very moment, and had your Opera box every night?

[She drinks champagne while talking, and excites herself.]

MISS PRIOR

Don't take that, mamma.

MRS PRIOR

Don't take it? why, it costs nothing; Milliken can afford it. Do you suppose I get champagne every day? I might have had it as a girl when I first married your father, and we kep' our gig and horse, and lived at Clapham, and had the best of everything. But the coal-trade is not what it was, Julia. We met with misfortunes, Julia, and we went into poverty: and your poor father went into the Bench for twenty-three months—two year all but a month he did—and my poor girl was obliged to dance at the "Coburg Theatre"—yes you were, at ten shillings a week, in the Oriental ballet of "The Bulbul and the Rose:" you were, my poor darling child.

MISS PRIOR

Hush, hush, mamma!

MRS PRIOR

And we kep' a lodging-house in Bury Street, St. James's, which your father's brother furnished for us, who was an extensive oil-merchant. He brought you up; and afterwards he quarrelled with my poor James, Robert Prior did, and he died, not leaving us a shilling. And my dear eldest boy went into a wine-merchant's office: and my poor darling Julia became a governess, when you had had the best of education at Clapham; you had, Julia. And to think that you were obliged, my blessed thing, to go on in the Oriental ballet of "The Rose and the Bul—"

MISS PRIOR

Mamma, hush, hush! forget that story.

[Enter **PAGE** from dining-room.

PAGE

Miss Prior! please, the ladies are coming from the dining-room. Mrs. B. have had her two glasses of port, and her ladyship is now a-telling the story about the Prince of Wales when she danced with him at Canton House.

[Exit **PAGE**.]

MISS PRIOR

Quick, quick! There, take your basket! Put on your bonnet, and good-night, mamma. Here, here is a half sovereign and three shillings; it is all the money I have in the world; take it, and buy the shoes for Adolphus.

MRS PRIOR

And the underclothing, my love—little Amelia's underclothing?

MISS PRIOR

We will see about it. Good-night—

[Kisses her].

Don't be seen here,—Lady K. doesn't like it.

[Enter **GENTLEMEN** and **LADIES** from dining-room.

LADY KICKLEBURY
We follow the Continental fashion. We don't sit after dinner, Captain Touchit.

CAPTAIN TOUCHIT
Confound the Continental fashion! I like to sit a little while after dinner [Aside].

MRS BONNINGTON
So does my dear Mr. Bonnington, Captain Touchit. He likes a little port-wine after dinner.

TOUCHIT
I'm not surprised at it, ma'am.

MRS BONNINGTON
When did you say your son was coming, Lady Kicklebury?

LADY KICKLEBURY
My Clarence! He will be here immediately, I hope, the dear boy. You know my Clarence?

TOUCHIT
Yes, ma'am.

LADY KICKLEBURY
And like him, I'm sure, Captain Touchit! Everybody does like Clarence Kicklebury.

TOUCHIT
The confounded young scamp! I say, Horace, do you like your brother-in-law?

MILLIKEN
Well—I—I can't say—I—like him—in fact, I don't. But that's no reason why his mother shouldn't.

[During this, **HOWELL**, preceded by **BULKELEY**, hands round coffee. The garden without has darkened, as if evening. **BULKELEY** is going away without offering coffee to **MISS PRIOR**. **JOHN** stamps on his foot, and points to her. **CAPTAIN TOUCHIT**, laughing, goes up and talks to her now the servants are gone.]

MRS BONNINGTON
Horace! I must tell you that the waste at your table is shocking. What is the need of opening all this wine? You and Lady Kicklebury were the only persons who took champagne.

TOUCHIT
I never drink it—never touch the rubbish! Too old a stager!

LADY KICKLEBURY
Port, I think, is your favorite, Mrs. Bonnington?

MRS BONNINGTON

My dear lady, I do not mean that you should not have champagne, if you like. Pray, pray, don't be angry! But why on earth, for you, who take so little, and Horace, who only drinks it to keep you company, should not Howell open a pint instead of a great large bottle?

LADY KICKLEBURY

Oh, Howell! Howell! We must not mention Howell, my dear Mrs. Bonnington. Howell is faultless! Howell has the keys of everything! Howell is not to be controlled in anything! Howell is to be at liberty to be rude to my servant!

MILLIKEN

Is that all? I am sure I should have thought your man was big enough to resent any rudeness from poor little Howell.

LADY KICKLEBURY

Horace! Excuse me for saying that you don't know—the—the class of servant to whom Bulkeley belongs. I had him, as a great favor, from Lord Toddleby. That class of servant is accustomed generally not to go out single.

MILLIKEN

Unless they are two behind a carriage-perch they pine away, as one love-bird does without his mate!

LADY KICKLEBURY

No doubt! no doubt! I only say you are not accustomed here—in this kind of establishment, you understand—to that class of—

MRS BONNINGTON

Lady Kicklebury! is my son's establishment not good enough for any powdered monster in England? Is the house of a British merchant—?

LADY KICKLEBURY

My dear creature! my dear creature! it IS the house of a British merchant, and a very comfortable house.

MRS BONNINGTON

Yes, as you find it.

LADY KICKLEBURY

Yes, as I find it, when I come to take care of my departed, angel's children, Mrs. Bonnington—

[Pointing to picture]

—of THAT dear seraph's orphans, Mrs. Bonnington. YOU cannot. You have other duties—other children—a husband at home in delicate health, who—

MRS BONNINGTON

Lady Kicklebury, no one shall say I don't take care of my dear husband!

MILLIKEN

My dear mother! My dear Lady Kicklebury! [To **TOUCHIT**, who has come forward.] They spar so every night they meet, Touchit. Ain't it hard?

LADY KICKLEBURY

I say you DO take care of Mr. Bonnington, Mrs. Bonnington, my dear creature! and that is why you can't attend to Horace. And as he is of a very easy temper—except sometimes with his poor Arabella's mother—he allows all his tradesmen to cheat him, all his servants to cheat him, Howell to be rude to everybody—to me amongst other people, and why not to my servant Bulkeley, with whom Lord Toddleby's groom of the chambers gave me the very highest character.

MRS BONNINGTON

I'm surprised that noblemen HAVE grooms in their chambers. I should think they were much better in the stables. I am sure I always think so when we dine with Doctor Clinker. His man does bring such a smell of the stable with him.

LADY KICKLEBURY

He! he! you mistake, my dearest creature! Your poor mother mistakes, my good Horace. You have lived in a quiet and most respectable sphere—but not—not—

MRS BONNINGTON

Not what, Lady Kicklebury? We have lived at Richmond twenty years—in my late husband's time—when we saw a great deal of company, and when this dear Horace was a dear boy at Westminster School. And we have PAID for everything we have had for twenty years, and we have owed not a penny to any TRADESMAN, though we mayn't have had POWDERED FOOTMEN SIX FEET HIGH, who were impertinent to all the maids in the place—Don't! I WILL speak, Horace—but servants who loved us, and who lived in our families.

MILLIKEN

Mamma, now, my dear, good old mother! I am sure Lady Kicklebury meant no harm.

LADY KICKLEBURY

Me! my dear Horace! harm! What harm could I mean?

MILLIKEN

Come! let us have a game at whist. Touchit, will you make a fourth? They go on so every night almost. Ain't it a pity, now?

TOUCHIT

Miss Prior generally plays, doesn't she?

MILLIKEN

And a very good player, too. But I thought you might like it.

TOUCHIT

Well, not exactly. I don't like sixpenny points, Horace, or quarrelling with old dragons about the odd trick. I will go and smoke a cigar on the terrace, and contemplate the silver Thames, the darkling woods, the starry hosts of heaven. I—I like smoking better than playing whist.

[**MILLIKEN** rings bell.]

MILLIKEN
Ah, George! you're not fit for domestic felicity.

TOUCHIT
No, not exactly.

[**HOWELL** enters.

MILLIKEN
Lights and a whist-table. Oh, I see you bring 'em. You know everything I want. He knows everything I want, Howell does. Let us cut. Miss Prior, you and I are partners!

ACT II

SCENE. As before.

LADY KICKLEBURY
Don't smoke, you naughty boy. I don't like it. Besides, it will encourage your brother-in-law to smoke.

CLARENCE KICKLEBURY
Anything to oblige you, I'm sure. But can't do without it, mother; it's good for my health. When I was in the Plungers, our doctor used to say, "You ought never to smoke more than eight cigars a day"—an order, you know, to do it—don't you see?

LADY KICKLEBURY
Ah, my child! I am very glad you are not with those unfortunate people in the East.

CLARENCE KICKLEBURY
So am I. Sold out just in time. Much better fun being here, than having the cholera at Scutari. Nice house, Milliken's. Snob, but good fellow—good cellar, doosid good cook. Really, that salmi yesterday,—couldn't have it better done at the "Rag" now. You have got into good quarters here, mother.

LADY KICKLEBURY
The meals are very good, and the house is very good; the manners are not of the first order. But what can you expect of city people? I always told your poor dear sister, when she married Mr. Milliken, that she might look for everything substantial,—but not manners. Poor dear Arabella WOULD marry him.

CLARENCE KICKLEBURY
Would! that is a good one, mamma! Why, you made her! It's a dozen years ago. But I recollect, when I came home from Eton, seeing her crying because Charley Tufton—

LADY KICKLEBURY

Mr. Tufton had not a shilling to bless himself with. The marriage was absurd and impossible.

CLARENCE KICKLEBURY
He hadn't a shilling then. I guess he has plenty now. Elder brother killed, out hunting. Father dead. Tuf a baronet, with four thousand a year if he's a shilling.

LADY KICKLEBURY
Not so much.

CLARENCE KICKLEBURY
Four thousand if it's a shilling. Why, the property adjoins Kicklebury's—I ought to know. I've shot over it a thousand times. Heh! I remember, when I was quite a young 'un, how Arabella used to go out into Tufton Park to meet Charley—and he is a doosid good fellow, and a gentlemanlike fellow, and a doosid deal better than this city fellow.

LADY KICKLEBURY
If you don't like this city fellow, Clarence, why do you come here? why didn't you stop with your elder brother at Kicklebury?

CLARENCE KICKLEBURY
Why didn't I? Why didn't YOU stop at Kicklebury, mamma? Because you had notice to quit. Serious daughter-in-law, quarrels about management of the house—row in the building. My brother interferes, and politely requests mamma to shorten her visit. So it is with your other two daughters; so it was with Arabella when she was alive. What shindies you used to have with her, Lady Kicklebury! Heh! I had a row with my brother and sister about a confounded little nursery-maid.

LADY KICKLEBURY
Clarence!

CLARENCE KICKLEBURY
And so I had notice to quit too. And I'm in very good quarters here, and I intend to stay in 'em, mamma. I say—

LADY KICKLEBURY
What do you say?

CLARENCE KICKLEBURY
Since I sold out, you know, and the regiment went abroad, confound me, the brutes at the "Rag" will hardly speak to me! I was so ill, I couldn't go. Who the doose can live the life I've led and keep health enough for that infernal Crimea? Besides, how could I help it? I was so cursedly in debt that I was OBLIGED to have the money, you know. YOU hadn't got any.

LADY KICKLEBURY
Not a halfpenny, my darling. I am dreadfully in debt myself.

CLARENCE KICKLEBURY
I know you are. So am I. My brother wouldn't give me any, not a dump. Hang him! Said he had his children to look to. Milliken wouldn't advance me any more—said I did him in that horse transaction.

He! he! he! so I did! What had I to do but to sell out? And the fellows cut me, by Jove. Ain't it too bad? I'll take my name off the "Rag," I will, though.

LADY KICKLEBURY

We must sow our wild oats, and we must sober down; and we must live here, where the living is very good and very cheap, Clarence, you naughty boy! And we must get you a rich wife. Did you see at church yesterday that young woman in light green, with rather red hair and a pink bonnet?

CLARENCE KICKLEBURY

I was asleep, ma'am, most of the time, or I was bookin' up the odds for the Chester Cup. When I'm bookin' up, I think of nothin' else, ma'am,—nothin'.

LADY KICKLEBURY

That was Miss Brocksopp—Briggs, Brown and Brocksopp, the great sugar-bakers. They say she will have eighty thousand pound. We will ask her to dinner here.

CLARENCE KICKLEBURY

I say—why the doose do you have such old women to dinner here? Why don't you get some pretty girls? Such a set of confounded old frumps as eat Milliken's mutton I never saw. There's you, and his old mother Mrs. Bonnington, and old Mrs. Fogram, and old Miss What's-her-name, the woman with the squint eye, and that immense Mrs. Crowder. It's so stoopid, that if it weren't for Touchit coming down sometimes, and the billiards and boatin', I should die here—expire, by gad! Why don't you have some pretty women into the house, Lady Kicklebury?

LADY KICKLEBURY

Why! Do you think I want that picture taken down: and another Mrs. Milliken? Wisehead! If Horace married again, would he be your banker, and keep this house, now that ungrateful son of mine has turned me out of his? No pretty woman shall come into the house whilst I am here.

CLARENCE KICKLEBURY

Governess seems a pretty woman: weak eyes, bad figure, poky, badly dressed, but doosid pretty woman.

LADY KICKLEBURY

Bah! There is no danger from HER. She is a most faithful creature, attached to me beyond everything. And her eyes—her eyes are weak with crying for some young man who is in India. She has his miniature in her room, locked up in one of her drawers.

CLARENCE KICKLEBURY

Then how the doose did you come to see it?

LADY KICKLEBURY

We see a number of things, Clarence. Will you drive with me?

CLARENCE KICKLEBURY

Not as I knows on, thank you. No, Ma; drivin's TOO slow: and you're goin' to call on two or three old dowagers in the Park? Thank your ladyship for the delightful offer.

[Enter **JOHN**.

JOHN
Please, sir, here's the man with the bill for the boats; two pound three.

CLARENCE KICKLEBURY
Damn it, pay it—don't bother ME!

JOHN
Haven't got the money, sir.

LADY KICKLEBURY
Howell! I saw Mr. Milliken give you a cheque for twenty-five pounds before he went into town this morning. Look sir

[Runs, opens drawer, takes out cheque-book].

There it is, marked, "Howell, 25L."

JOHN
Would your ladyship like to step down into my pantry and see what I've paid with the twenty-five pounds? Did my master leave any orders that your ladyship was to inspect my accounts?

LADY KICKLEBURY
Step down into the pantry! inspect your accounts? I never heard such impertinence. What do you mean, sir?

CLARENCE KICKLEBURY
Dammy, sir, what do you mean?

JOHN
I thought as her ladyship kept a heye over my master's private book, she might like to look at mine too.

LADY KICKLEBURY
Upon my word, this insolence is too much.

JOHN
I beg your ladyship's pardon. I am sure I have said nothing.

CLARENCE KICKLEBURY
Said, sir! your manner is mutinous, by Jove, sir! if I had you in the regiment!—

JOHN
I understood that you had left the regiment, sir, just before it went on the campaign, sir.

CLARENCE KICKLEBURY
Confound you, sir!

[Starts up.]

LADY KICKLEBURY

Clarence, my child, my child!

JOHN

Your ladyship needn't be alarmed; I'm a little man, my lady, but I don't think Mr. Clarence was a-goin' for to hit me, my lady; not before a lady, I'm sure. I suppose, sir, that you WON'T pay the boatman?

CLARENCE KICKLEBURY

No, sir, I won't pay him, nor any man who uses this sort of damned impertinence!

JOHN

I told Rullocks, sir, I thought it was JEST possible you wouldn't.

[Exit.]

CLARENCE KICKLEBURY

That's a nice man, that is—an impudent villain!

LADY KICKLEBURY

Ruined by Horace's weakness. He ruins everybody, poor good-natured Horace!

CLARENCE KICKLEBURY

Why don't you get rid of the blackguard?

LADY KICKLEBURY

There is a time for all things, my dear. This man is very convenient to Horace. Mr. Milliken is exceedingly lazy, and Howell spares him a great deal of trouble. Some day or other I shall take all this domestic trouble off his hands. But not yet: your poor brother-in-law is restive, like many weak men. He is subjected to other influences: his odious mother thwarts me a great deal.

CLARENCE KICKLEBURY

Why, you used to be the dearest friends in the world. I recollect when I was at Eton—

LADY KICKLEBURY

Were; but friendship don't last for ever. Mrs. Bonnington and I have had serious differences since I came to live here: she has a natural jealousy, perhaps, at my superintending her son's affairs. When she ceases to visit at the house, as she very possibly will, things will go more easily; and Mr. Howell will go too, you may depend upon it. I am always sorry when my temper breaks out, as it will sometimes.

CLARENCE KICKLEBURY

Won't it, that's all!

LADY KICKLEBURY

At his insolence, my temper is high; so is yours, my dear. Calm it for the present, especially as regards Howell.

CLARENCE KICKLEBURY
Gad! d'you know I was very nearly pitching into him? But once, one night in the Haymarket, at a lobster-shop, where I was with some fellows, we chaffed some other fellows, and there was one fellah—quite a little fellah—and I pitched into him, and he gave me the most confounded lickin' I ever had in my life, since my brother Kicklebury licked me when we were at Eton; and that, you see, was a lesson to me, ma'am. Never trust those little fellows, never chaff 'em: dammy, they may be boxers.

LADY KICKLEBURY
You quarrelsome boy! I remember you coming home with your naughty head SO bruised.

[Looks at watch.]

I must go now to take my drive.

[Exit **LADY KICKLEBURY**]

CLARENCE KICKLEBURY
I owe a doose of a tick at that billiard-room; I shall have that boatman dunnin' me. Why hasn't Milliken got any horses to ride? Hang him! suppose he can't ride—suppose he's a tailor. He ain't MY tailor, though, though I owe him a doosid deal of money. There goes mamma with that darling nephew and niece of mine.

[Enter **BULKELEY**].

Why haven't you gone with my lady, you, sir? [to **BULKELEY**.]

BULKELEY
My lady have a-took the pony-carriage, sir; Mrs. Bonnington have a-took the hopen carriage and 'orses, sir, this mornin', which the Bishop of London is 'olding a confirmation at Teddington, sir, and Mr. Bonnington is attending the serimony. And I have told Mr. 'Owell, sir, that my lady would prefer the hopen carriage, sir, which I like the hexercise myself, sir, and that the pony-carriage was good enough for Mrs. Bonnington, sir; and Mr. 'Owell was very hinsolent to me, sir; and I don't think I can stay in the 'ouse with him.

CLARENCE KICKLEBURY
Hold your jaw, sir.

BULKELEY
Yes, sir.

[Exit **BULKELEY**.]

CLARENCE KICKLEBURY
I wonder who that governess is?—sang rather prettily last night—wish she'd come and sing now—wish she'd come and amuse me—I've seen her face before—where have I seen her face?—it ain't at all a bad one. What shall I do? dammy, I'll read a book: I've not read a book this ever so long. What's here?

[Looks amongst books, selects one, sinks down in easy-chair so as quite to be lost.]

[Enter **MISS PRIOR**.

MISS PRIOR

There's peace in the house! those noisy children are away with their grandmamma. The weather is beautiful, and I hope they will take a long drive. Now I can have a quiet half-hour, and finish that dear pretty "Ruth"—oh, how it makes me cry, that pretty story.

[Lays down her bonnet on table—goes to glass—takes off cap and spectacles—arranges her hair—**CLARENCE** has got on chair looking at her.]

CLARENCE KICKLEBURY

By Jove! I know who it is now! Remember her as well as possible. Four years ago, when little Foxbury used to dance in the ballet over the water. DON'T I remember her! She boxed my ears behind the scenes, by jingo.

[Coming forward]

Miss Pemberton! Star of the ballet! Light of the harem! Don't you remember the grand Oriental ballet of the "Bulbul and the Peri?"

MISS PRIOR

Oh! [Screams.] No, n—no, sir. You are mistaken: my name is Prior. I—never was at the "Coburg Theatre." I—

CLARENCE KICKLEBURY [Seizing her hand]

No, you don't, though! What! don't you remember well that little hand slapping this face? which nature hadn't then adorned with whiskers, by gad! You pretend you have forgotten little Foxbury, whom Charley Calverley used to come after, and who used to drive to the "Coburg" every night in her brougham. How did you know it was the "Coburg?" That IS a good one! HAD you there, I think.

MISS PRIOR

Sir, in the name of heaven, pity me! I have to keep my mother and my sisters and my brothers. When—when you saw me, we were in great poverty; and almost all the wretched earnings I made at that time were given to my poor father then lying in the Queen's Bench hard by. You know there was nothing against my character—you know there was not. Ask Captain Touchit whether I was not a good girl. It was he who brought me to this house.

CLARENCE KICKLEBURY

Touchit! the old villain!

MISS PRIOR

I had your sister's confidence. I tended her abroad on her death-bed. I have brought up your nephew and niece. Ask any one if I have not been honest? As a man, as a gentleman, I entreat you to keep my secret! I implore you for the sake of my poor mother and her children!

[Kneeling.]

CLARENCE KICKLEBURY

By Jove! how handsome you are! How crying becomes your eyes! Get up; get up. Of course I'll keep your secret, but—

MISS PRIOR

Ah! ah!

[She screams as he tries to embrace her. **HOWELL** rushes in.]

HOWELL

Hands off, you little villain! Stir a step and I'll kill you, if you were a regiment of captains! What! insult this lady who kept watch at your sister's death-bed and has took charge of her children! Don't be frightened, Miss Prior. Julia—dear, dear Julia—I'm by you. If the scoundrel touches you, I'll kill him. I—I love you—there—it's here—love you madly—with all my 'art—my a-heart!

MISS PRIOR

Howell—for heaven's sake, Howell!

CLARENCE KICKLEBURY

Pooh—ooh! [Bursting with laughter]. Here's a novel, by jingo! Here's John in love with the governess. Fond of plush, Miss Pemberton—ey? Gad, it's the best thing I ever knew. Saved a good bit, ey, Jeames? Take a public-house? By Jove! I'll buy my beer there.

JOHN

Owe for it, you mean. I don't think your tradesmen profit much by your custom, ex-Cornet Kicklebury.

CLARENCE KICKLEBURY

By Jove! I'll do for you, you villain!

JOHN

No, not that way, Captain.

[Struggles with and throws him.]

CLARENCE KICKLEBURY [Screams.]

Hallo, Bulkeley!

[**BULKELEY** is seen strolling in the garden.]

[Enter **BULKELEY.**

BULKELEY

What is it, sir?

CLARENCE KICKLEBURY

Take this confounded villain off me, and pitch him into the Thames—do you hear?

JOHN

Come here, and I'll break every bone in your hulking body. [To **BULKELEY**.]

BULKELEY
Come, come! whatever his hall this year row about?

MISS PRIOR
For heaven's sake don't strike that poor man.

BULKELEY
YOU be quiet. What's he a-hittin' about my master for?

JOHN
Take off your hat, sir, when you speak to a lady.

[Takes up a poker.]

And now come on, both of you, cowards!

[Rushes at **BULKELEY** and knocks his hat off his head.]

BULKELEY [Stepping back]
If you'll put down that there poker, you know, then I'll pitch into you fast enough. But that there poker ain't fair, you know.

CLARENCE KICKLEBURY
You villain! of course you will leave this house. And, Miss Prior, I think you understand that you will go too. I don't think my niece wants to learn DANCIN', you understand. Good-by. Here, Bulkeley!

[Gets behind **FOOTMAN** and exit.]

MISS PRIOR
Do you know the meaning of that threat, Mr. Howell?

JOHN
Yes, Miss Prior.

MISS PRIOR
I was a dancer once, for three months, four years ago, when my poor father was in prison.

JOHN
Yes, Miss Prior, I knew it. And I saw you a many times.

MISS PRIOR
And you kept my secret?

JOHN
Yes, Ju—Jul—Miss Prior.

MISS PRIOR

Thank you, and God bless you, John Howell. There, there. You mustn't! indeed you mustn't!

JOHN

You don't remember the printer's boy who used to come to Mr. O'Reilly, and sit in your 'all in Bury Street, Miss Prior? I was that boy. I was a country-bred boy—that is if you call Putney country, and Wimbledon Common and that. I served the Milliken family seven year. I went with Master Horace to college, and then I revolted against service, and I thought I'd be a man and turn printer like Doctor Frankling. And I got in an office: and I went with proofs to Mr. O'Reilly, and I saw you. And though I might have been in love with somebody else before I did—yet it was all hup when I saw you.

MISS PRIOR [Kindly]

YOU must not talk to me in that way, John Howell.

JOHN

Let's tell the tale out. I couldn't stand the newspaper night-work. I had a mother and brothers and sisters to keep, as you had. I went back to Horace Milliken and said, Sir, I've lost my work. I and mine want bread. Will you take me back again? And he did. He's a kind, kind soul is my master.

MISS PRIOR

He IS a kind, kind soul.

JOHN

He's good to all the poor. His hand's in his pocket for everybody. Everybody takes advantage of him. His mother-in-lor rides over him. So does his Ma. So do I, I may say; but that's over now; and you and I have had our notice to quit. Miss, I should say.

MISS PRIOR

Yes.

JOHN

I have saved a bit of money—not much—a hundred pound. Miss Prior—Julia—here I am—look—I'm a poor feller—a poor servant—but I've the heart of a man—and—I love you—oh! I love you!

MARY

Oh ho—ho!

[**MARY** has entered from garden, and bursts out crying.]

MISS PRIOR

It can't be, John Howell—my dear, brave, kind John Howell. It can't be. I have watched this for some time past, and poor Mary's despair here.

[Kisses **MARY**, who cries plentifully.]

You have the heart of a true, brave man, and must show it and prove it now. I am not—am not of your pardon me for saying so—of your class in life. I was bred by my uncle, away from my poor parents, though I came back to them after his sudden death; and to poverty, and to this dependent life I am now leading. I am a servant, like you, John, but in another sphere—have to seek another place now; and heaven knows if I shall procure one, now that that unlucky passage in my life is known. Oh, the coward to recall it! the coward!

MARY
But John whopped him, Miss! that he did. He gave it him well, John did. [Crying.]

MISS PRIOR
You can't—you ought not to forego an attachment like that, John Howell. A more honest and true-hearted creature never breathed than Mary Barlow.

JOHN
No, indeed.

MISS PRIOR
She has loved you since she was a little child. And you loved her once, and do now, John.

MARY
Oh, Miss! you hare a hangel,—I hallways said you were a hangel.

MISS PRIOR
You are better than I am, my dear much, much better than I am, John. The curse of my poverty has been that I have had to flatter and to dissemble, and hide the faults of those I wanted to help, and to smile when I was hurt, and laugh when I was sad, and to coax, and to tack, and to bide my time,—not with Mr. Milliken: he is all honor, and kindness, and simplicity. Who did HE ever injure, or what unkind word did HE ever say? But do you think, with the jealousy of those poor ladies over his house, I could have stayed here without being a hypocrite to both of them? Go, John. My good, dear friend, John Howell, marry Mary. You'll be happier with her than with me. There! There!

[They embrace.]

MARY
O—o—o! I think I'll go and hiron hout Miss Harabella's frocks now.

[Exit **MARY**.]

[Enter **MILLIKEN** with **CLARENCE KICKLEBURY**—who is explaining things to him.

CLARENCE KICKLEBURY
Here they are, I give you my word of honor. Ask 'em, damn em.

MILLIKEN
What is this I hear? You, John Howell, have dared to strike a gentleman under my roof! Your master's brother-in-law?

JOHN
Yes, by Jove! and I'd do it again.

MILLIKEN

Are you drunk or mad, Howell?

JOHN

I'm as sober and as sensible as ever I was in my life, sir—I not only struck the master, but I struck the man, who's twice as big, only not quite as big a coward, I think.

MILLIKEN

Hold your scurrilous tongues sir! My good nature ruins everybody about me. Make up your accounts. Pack your trunks—and never let me see your face again.

JOHN

Very good, sir.

MILLIKEN

I suppose, Miss Prior, you will also be disposed to—to follow Mr. Howell?

MISS PRIOR

To quit you, now you know what has passed? I never supposed it could be otherwise—I deceived you, Mr. Milliken—as I kept a secret from you, and must pay the penalty. It is a relief to me, the sword has been hanging over me. I wish I had told your poor wife, as I was often minded to do.

MILLIKEN

Oh, you were minded to do it in Italy, were you?

MISS PRIOR

Captain Touchit knew it, sir, all along: and that my motives and, thank God, my life were honorable.

MILLIKEN

Oh, Touchit knew it, did he? and thought it honorable—honorable. Ha! ha! to marry a footman—and keep a public-house? I—I beg your pardon, John Howell—I mean nothing against you, you know. You're an honorable man enough, except that you have been damned Insolent to my brother-in-law.

JOHN

Oh, heaven!

[**JOHN** strikes his forehead, and walks away.]

MISS PRIOR

You mistake me, sir. What I wished to speak of was the fact which this gentleman has no doubt communicated to you—that I danced on the stage for three months.

MILLIKEN

Oh, yes. Oh, damme, yes. I forgot. I wasn't thinking of that.

CLARENCE KICKLEBURY

You see she owns it.

MISS PRIOR

We were in the depths of poverty. Our furniture and lodging-house under execution—from which Captain Touchit, when he came to know of our difficulties, nobly afterwards released us. My father was in prison, and wanted shillings for medicine, and I—I went and danced on the stage.

MILLIKEN

Well?

MISS PRIOR

And I kept the secret afterwards; knowing that I could never hope as governess to obtain a place after having been a stage-dancer.

MILLIKEN

Of course you couldn't,—it's out of the question; and may I ask, are you going to resume that delightful profession when you enter the married state with Mr. Howell?

MISS PRIOR

Poor John! it is not I who am going to—that is, it's Mary, the school-room maid.

MILLIKEN

Eternal blazes! Have you turned Mormon, John Howell, and are you going to marry the whole house?

JOHN

I made a hass of myself about Miss Prior. I couldn't help her being I—I—lovely.

CLARENCE KICKLEBURY

Gad, he proposed to her in my presence.

JOHN

What I proposed to her, Cornet Clarence Kicklebury, was my heart and my honor, and my best, and my everything—and you—you wanted to take advantage of her secret, and you offered her indignities, and you laid a cowardly hand on her—a cowardly hand!—and I struck you, and I'd do it again.

MILLIKEN

What? Is this true?

[Turning round very fiercely to **CLARENCE KICKLEBURY**]

CLARENCE KICKLEBURY

Gad! Well—I only—

MILLIKEN

You only what? You only insulted a lady under my roof—the friend and nurse of your dead sister—the guardian of my children. You only took advantage of a defenceless girl, and would have extorted your infernal pay out of her fear. You miserable sneak and coward!

CLARENCE KICKLEBURY

Hallo! Come, come! I say I won't stand this sort of chaff. Dammy, I'll send a friend to you!

MILLIKEN

Go out of that window, sir. March! or I will tell my servant, John Howell, to kick you out, you wretched little scamp! Tell that big brute,—what's-his-name?—Lady Kicklebury's man, to pack this young man's portmanteau and bear's-grease pots; and if ever you enter these doors again, Clarence Kicklebury, by the heaven that made me!—by your sister who is dead!—I will cane your life out of your bones. Angel in heaven! Shade of my Arabella—to think that your brother in your house should be found to insult the guardian of your children!

JOHN

By jingo, you're a good-plucked one! I knew he was, Miss,—I told you he was.

[Exit, shaking hands with his **MASTER**, and with **MISS PRIOR**, and dancing for joy. Exit **CLARENCE**, scared, out of window.]

JOHN [Without]

Bulkeley! pack up the Capting's luggage!

MILLIKEN

How can I ask your pardon, Miss Prior? In my wife's name I ask it—in the name of that angel whose dying-bed you watched and soothed—of the innocent children whom you have faithfully tended since.

MISS PRIOR

Ah, sir! it is granted when you speak so to me.

MILLIKEN

Eh, eh—d—don't call me sir!

MISS PRIOR

It is for me to ask pardon for hiding what you know now: but if I had told you—you—you never would have taken me into your house—your wife never would.

MILLIKEN

No, no. [Weeping.]

MISS PRIOR

My dear, kind Captain Touchit knows it all. It was by his counsel I acted. He it was who relieved our distress. Ask him whether my conduct was not honorable—ask him whether my life was not devoted to my parents—ask him when—when I am gone.

MILLIKEN

When you are gone, Julia! Why are you going? Why should you go, my love—that is—why need you go, in the devil's name?

MISS PRIOR

Because, when your mother—when your mother-in-law come to hear that your children's governess has been a dancer on the stage, they will send me away, and you will not have the power to resist them.

They ought to send me away, sir; but I have acted honestly by the children and their poor mother, and you'll think of me kindly when—I—am—gone?

MILLIKEN
Julia, my dearest—dear—noble—dar—the devil! here's old Kicklebury.

Enter **LADY KICKLEBURY, CHILDREN,** and **CLARENCE KICKLEBURY.**

LADY KICKLEBURY
So, Miss Prior! this is what I hear, is it? A dancer in my house! a serpent in my bosom—poisoning—yes, poisoning those blessed children! occasioning quarrels between my own son and my dearest son-in-law; flirting with the footman! When do you intend to leave, madam, the house which you have po—poll—luted?

MISS PRIOR
I need no hard language, Lady Kicklebury: and I will reply to none. I have signified to Mr. Milliken my wish to leave his house.

MILLIKEN
Not, not, if you will stay. [To **MISS PRIOR**]

LADY KICKLEBURY
Stay, Horace! she shall NEVER stay as governess in this house!

MILLIKEN
Julia! will you stay as mistress? You have known me for a year alone—before, not so well—when the house had a mistress that is gone. You know what my temper is, and that my tastes are simple, and my heart not unkind. I have watched you, and have never seen you out of temper, though you have been tried. I have long thought you good and beautiful, but I never thought to ask the question which I put to you now:—come in, sir! [To **CLARENCE** at door]:—now that you have been persecuted by those who ought to have upheld you, and insulted by those who owed you gratitude and respect. I am tired of their domination, and as weary of a man's cowardly impertinence [To **CLARENCE**] as of a woman's jealous tyranny. They have made what was my Arabella's home miserable by their oppression and their quarrels. Julia! my wife's friend, my children's friend! be mine, and make me happy! Don't leave me, Julia! say you won't—say you won't—dearest—dearest girl!

MISS PRIOR
I won't—leave—you.

GEORGE [Without]
Oh, I say! Arabella, look here: here's papa a-kissing Miss Prior!

LADY KICKLEBURY
Horace—Clarence my son! Shade of my Arabella! can you behold this horrible scene, and not shudder in heaven! Bulkeley! Clarence! go for a doctor—go to Doctor Straitwaist at the Asylum—Horace Milliken, who has married the descendant of the Kickleburys of the Conqueror, marry a dancing-girl off the stage! Horace Milliken! do you wish to see me die in convulsions at your feet? I writhe there, I grovel there. Look! look at me on my knees! your own mother-in-law! drive away this fiend!

MILLIKEN

Hem! I ought to thank you, Lady Kicklebury, for it is you that have given her to me.

LADY KICKLEBURY

He won't listen! he turns away and kisses her horrible hand. This will never do: help me up, Clarence, I must go and fetch his mother. Ah, ah! there she is, there she is!

[**LADY KICKLEBURY** rushes out, as the top of a barouche, with **MR** and **MRS BONNINGTON** and **COACHMAN**, is seen over the gate.]

MRS BONNINGTON

What is this I hear, my son, my son? You are going to marry a—a stage-dancer? you are driving me mad, Horace!

MILLIKEN

Give me my second chance, mother, to be happy. You have had yourself two chances.

MRS BONNINGTON

Speak to him, Mr. Bonnington.

[**MRS BONNINGTON** makes dumb show.]

LADY KICKLEBURY

Implore him, Mr. Bonnington.

MRS BONNINGTON

Pray, pray for him, Mr. Bonnington, my love—my lost, abandoned boy!

LADY KICKLEBURY

Oh, my poor dear Mrs. Bonnington!

MRS BONNINGTON

Oh, my poor dear Lady Kicklebury.

[They embrace each other.]

LADY KICKLEBURY

I have been down on my knees to him, dearest Mrs. Bonnington.

MRS BONNINGTON

Let us both—both go down on our knees—I WILL [To her **HUSBAND**]. Edward, I will!

[Both **LADIES** on their knees. **BONNINGTON** with outstretched hands behind them.]

Look, unhappy boy! look, Horace! two mothers on their wretched knees before you, imploring you to send away this monster! Speak to him, Mr. Bonnington. Edward! use authority with him, if he will not listen to his mother—

LADY KICKLEBURY
To his mothers!

[Enter **TOUCHIT**.

TOUCHIT
What is this comedy going on, ladies and gentlemen? The ladies on their elderly knees—Miss Prior with her hair down her back. Is it tragedy or comedy—is it a rehearsal for a charade, or are we acting for Horace's birthday? or, oh!—I beg your Reverence's pardon—you were perhaps going to a professional duty?

MR BONNINGTON
It's WE who are praying this child, Touchit. This child, with whom you used to come home from Westminster when you were boys. You have influence with him; he listens to you. Entreat him to pause in his madness.

TOUCHIT
What madness?

MRS BONNINGTON
That—that woman—that serpent yonder—that—that dancing-woman, whom you introduced to Arabella Milliken,—ah! and I rue the day:—Horace is going to mum—mum—marry her!

TOUCHIT
Well! I always thought he would. Ever since I saw him and her playing at whist together, when I came down here a month ago, I thought he would do it.

MRS BONNINGTON
Oh, it's the whist, the whist! Why did I ever play at whist, Edward? My poor Mr. Milliken used to like his rubber.

TOUCHIT
Since he has been a widower—

LADY KICKLEBURY
A widower of that angel!

[Points to picture.]

TOUCHIT
Pooh, pooh, angel! You two ladies have never given the poor fellow any peace. You were always quarrelling over him. You took possession of his house, bullied his servants, spoiled his children; you did, Lady Kicklebury.

LADY KICKLEBURY
Sir, you are a rude, low, presuming, vulgar man. Clarence! beat this rude man!

TOUCHIT
From what I have heard of your amiable son, he is not in the warlike line, I think. My dear Julia, I am delighted with all my heart that my old friend should have found a woman of sense, good conduct, good temper—a woman who has had many trials, and borne them with great patience—to take charge of him and make him happy. Horace, give me your hand! I knew Miss Prior in great poverty. I am sure she will bear as nobly her present good fortune; for good fortune it is to any woman to become the wife of such a loyal, honest, kindly gentleman as you are!

[Enter **JOHN**.

JOHN
If you please, my lady—if you please, sir—Bulkeley—

LADY KICKLEBURY
What of Bulkeley, sir?

JOHN
He has packed his things, and Cornet Kicklebury's things, my lady.

MILLIKEN
Let the fellow go.

JOHN
He won't go, sir, till my lady have paid him his book and wages. Here's the book, sir.

LADY KICKLEBURY
Insolence! quit my presence! And I, Mr. Milliken, will quit a house—

JOHN
Shall I call your ladyship a carriage?

LADY KICKLEBURY
Where I have met with rudeness, cruelty, and fiendish—

[To **MISS PRIOR**, who smiles and curtsies]

—yes, fiendish ingratitude. I will go, I say, as soon as I have made arrangements for taking other lodgings. You cannot expect a lady of fashion to turn out like a servant.

JOHN
Hire the "Star and Garter" for her, sir. Send down to the "Castle;" anything to get rid of her. I'll tell her maid to pack her traps. Pinhorn!

[Beckons **MAID** and gives orders.]

TOUCHIT
You had better go at once, my dear Lady Kicklebury.

LADY KICKLEBURY
Sir!

TOUCHIT
THE OTHER MOTHER-IN-LAW IS COMING! I met her on the road with all her family. He! he! he!
[Screams.]

[Enter **MRS PRIOR** and **CHILDREN**.

MRS PRIOR
My lady! I hope your ladyship is quite well! Dear, kind Mrs. Bonnington! I came to pay my duty to you, ma'am. This is Charlotte, my lady—the great girl whom your ladyship so kindly promised the gown for; and this is my little girl, Mrs. Bonnington, ma'am, please; and this is my Bluecoat boy. Go and speak to dear, kind Mr. Milliken—our best friend and protector—the son and son-in-law of these dear ladies. Look, sir! He has brought his copy to show you.

[**BOY** shows copy.]

Ain't it creditable to a boy of his age, Captain Touchit? And my best and most grateful services to you, sir. Julia, Julia, my dear, where's your cap and spectacles, you stupid thing? You've let your hair drop down. What! what!—

[Begins to be puzzled.]

MRS BONNINGTON
Is this collusion, madam?

MRS PRIOR
Collusion, dear Mrs. Bonnington!

LADY KICKLEBURY
Or insolence, Mrs. Prior!

MRS PRIOR
Insolence, your ladyship! What—what is it? what has happened? What's Julia's hair down for? Ah! you've not sent the poor girl away? the poor, poor child, and the poor, poor children!

TOUCHIT
That dancing at the "Coburg" has come out, Mrs. Prior.

MRS PRIOR
Not the darling's fault. It was to help her poor father in prison. It was I who forced her to do it. Oh! don't, don't, dear Lady Kicklebury, take the bread out of the mouths of these poor orphans! [Crying.]

MILLIKEN
Enough of this, Mrs. Prior: your daughter is not going away. Julia has promised to stay with me—and—never to leave me—as governess no longer, but as wife to me.

MRS PRIOR

Is it—is it true, Julia?

MISS PRIOR

Yes, mamma.

MRS PRIOR

Oh! oh! oh!

[Flings down her umbrella, kisses **JULIA**, and running to **MILLIKEN**,]

My son, my son! Come here, children. Come, Adolphus, Amelia, Charlotte—kiss your dear brother, children. What, my dears! How do you do, dears? [to **MILLIKEN'S CHILDREN**]. Have they heard the news? And do you know that my daughter is going to be your mamma? There—there—go and play with your little uncles and aunts, that's good children!

[She motions off the **CHILDREN**, who retire towards garden. Her manner changes to one of great patronage and intense satisfaction.]

Most hot weather, your ladyship, I'm sure. Mr. Bonnington, you must find it hot weather for preachin'! Lor'! there's that little wretch beatin' Adolphus! George, sir! have done, sir!

[Runs to separate them.]

How ever shall we make those children agree, Julia?

MISS PRIOR

They have been a little spoiled, and I think Mr. Milliken will send George and Arabella to school, mamma: will you not, Horace?

MR MILLIKEN

I think school will be the very best thing for them.

MRS PRIOR

And—

[**MRS PRIOR** whispers, pointing to her own children]

—the blue room, the green room, the rooms old Lady Kick has—plenty of room for us, my dear!

MISS PRIOR

No, mamma, I think it will be too large a party,—Mr. Milliken has often said that he would like to go abroad, and I hope that now he will be able to make his tour.

MRS PRIOR

Oh, then! we can live in the house, you know: what's the use of payin' lodgin', my dear!

MISS PRIOR

The house is going to be painted. You had best live in your own house, mamma; and if you want anything, Horace, Mr. Milliken, I am sure, will make it comfortable for you. He has had too many visitors of late, and will like a more quiet life, I think. Will you not?

MILLIKEN
I shall like a life with YOU, Julia.

JOHN
Cab, sir, for her ladyship!

LADY KICKLEBURY
This instant let me go! Call my people. Clarence, your arm! Bulkeley, Pinhorn! Mrs. Bonnington, I wish you good-morning! Arabella, angel!

[Looks at picture]

I leave you. I shall come to you ere long.

[Exit, refusing **MILLIKEN's** hand, passes up garden, with her **SERVANTS** following her. **MARY** and other **SERVANTS** of the house are collected together, whom **LADY KICKLEBURY** waves off. Bluecoat **BOY** on wall eating plums. Page, as she goes, cries, Hurray, hurray! Bluecoat boy cries, Hurray! When **LADY KICKLEBURY** is gone, **JOHN** advances.]

JOHN
I think I heard you say, sir, that it was your intention to go abroad?

MILLIKEN
Yes; oh, yes! Are we going abroad, my Julia?

MISS PRIOR
To settle matters, to have the house painted, and clear—

[Pointing to children, mother, &c.]

Don't you think it is the best thing that we can do?

MILLIKEN
Surely, surely: we are going abroad. Howell, you will come with us of course, and with your experiences you will make a capital courier. Won't Howell make a capital courier, Julia? Good honest fellow, John Howell. Beg your pardon for being so rude to you just now. But my temper is very hot, very.

JOHN [Laughing]
You are a Tartar, sir. Such a tyrant! isn't he, ma'am?

MISS PRIOR
Well, no; I don't think you have a very bad temper, Mr. Milliken, a—Horace.

JOHN

You must—take care of him—alone, Miss Prior—Julia—I mean Mrs. Milliken. Man and boy I've waited on him this fifteen year: with the exception of that trial at the printing-office, which—which I won't talk of NOW, madam. I never knew him angry; though many a time I have known him provoked. I never knew him say a hard word, though sometimes perhaps we've deserved it. Not often—such a good master as that is pretty sure of getting a good servant—that is, if a man has a heart in his bosom; and these things are found both in and out of livery. Yes, I have been a honest servant to him,—haven't I, Mr. Milliken?

MILLIKEN
Indeed, yes, John.

JOHN
And so has Mary Barlow. Mary, my dear!

[**MARY** comes forward.]

Will you allow me to introduce you, sir, to the futur' Mrs. Howell?—if Mr. Bonnington does YOUR little business for you, as I dare say—

[Turning to **MR BONNINGTON**]

—hold gov'nor, you will!—Make it up with your poor son, Mrs. Bonnington, ma'am. You have took a second 'elpmate, why shouldn't Master Horace? [To **MRS BONNINGTON**] He—he wants somebody to help him, and take care of him, more than you do.

TOUCHIT
You never spoke a truer word in your life, Howell.

JOHN
It's my general 'abit, Capting, to indulge in them sort of statements. A true friend I have been to my master, and a true friend I'll remain when he's my master no more.

MILLIKEN
Why, John, you are not going to leave me?

JOHN
It's best, sir, I should go. I—I'm not fit to be a servant in this house any longer. I wish to sit in my own little home, with my own little wife by my side. Poor dear! you've no conversation, Mary, but you're a good little soul. We've saved a hundred pound apiece, and if we want more, I know who won't grudge it us, a good fellow—a good master—for whom I've saved many a hundred pound myself, and will take the "Milliken Arms" at old Pigeoncot—and once a year or so, at this hanniversary, we will pay our respects to you, sir, and madam. Perhaps we will bring some children with us, perhaps we will find some more in this villa. Bless 'em beforehand! Good-by, sir, and madam—come away, Mary!

[Going].

MRS PRIOR [Entering with clothes, &c.]

She has not left a single thing in her room. Amelia, come here! this cloak will do capital for you, and this—this garment is the very thing for Adolphus. Oh, John! eh, Howell! will you please to see that my children have something to eat, immediately! The Milliken children, I suppose, have dined already?

JOHN
Yes, ma'am; certainly, ma'am.

MRS PRIOR
I see he is inclined to be civil to me NOW!

MISS PRIOR
John Howell is about to leave us, mamma. He is engaged to Mary Barlow, and when we go away, he is going to set up housekeeping for himself. Good-by, and thank you, John Howell—

[Gives her hand to **JOHN**, but with great reserve of manner].

You have been a kind and true friend to us—if ever we can serve you, count upon us—may he not, Mr. Milliken?

MILLIKEN
Always, always.

MISS PRIOR
But you will still wait upon us—upon Mr. Milliken, for a day or two, won't you, John, until we—until Mr. Milliken has found some one to replace you. He will never find any one more honest than you, and good, kind little Mary. Thank you, Mary, for your goodness to the poor governess.

MARY
Oh miss! oh mum!

[**MISS PRIOR** kisses **MARY** patronizingly].

MISS PRIOR [To **JOHN**]
And after they have had some refreshment, get a cab for my brothers and sister, if you please, John. Don't you think that will be best, my—my dear?

MILLIKEN
Of course, of course, dear Julia!

MISS PRIOR
And, Captain Touchit, you will stay, I hope, and dine with Mr. Milliken? And, Mrs. Bonnington, if you will receive as a daughter one who has always had a sincere regard for you, I think you will aid in making your son happy, as I promise you with all my heart and all my life to endeavor to do.

[**MISS PRIOR** and **MILLIKEN** go up to **MRS BONNINGTON**.]

MRS BONNINGTON
Well, there, then, since it must be so, bless you, my children.

TOUCHIT

Spoken like a sensible woman! And now, as I do not wish to interrupt this felicity, I will go and dine at the "Star and Garter."

MISS PRIOR

My dear Captain Touchit, not for worlds! Don't you know I mustn't be alone with Mr. Milliken until—until—?

MILLIKEN

Until I am made the happiest man alive! and you will come down and see us often, Touchit, won't you? And we hope to see our friends here often. And we will have a little life and spirit and gayety in the place. Oh, mother! oh, George! oh, Julia! what a comfort it is to me to think that I am released from the tyranny of that terrible mother-in-law!

MRS PRIOR

Come in to your teas, children. Come this moment, I say.

[The **CHILDREN** pass quarrelling behind the characters, **MRS PRIOR** summoning them; **JOHN** and **MARY** standing on each side of the dining-room door, as the curtain falls.]

William Makepeace Thackeray – A Short Biography

William Makepeace Thackeray, was born on July 18th, 1811 in Calcutta, then British India, where his father, Richmond Thackeray was the secretary to the Board of Revenue in the British East India Company. His mother, Anne Becher also worked for the British East India Company.

His father died in 1815, and his mother sent Thackeray to England the following year while she remained in India and would, sometime later, marry her childhood sweetheart. En-route to England the ship stopped for provisions on St. Helena. The Imprisoned Napoleon was pointed out to him by a servant with the words that he "eats three sheep every day, and all the little children he can lay hands on!"

Finally, back in England the young Thackeray was sent to school, initially in Southampton and Chiswick, before being moved to Charterhouse School. Charterhouse and Thackeray did not take to each other but the time became a valuable source for his later work "Slaughterhouse". Despite his less than respectful recalling of his time with them Charterhouse placed a monument in the chapel after his death.

In his final year at Charterhouse a troubling illness delayed his departure to attend Cambridge University. Over the course of his life Thackeray would suffer from ill health, much of it brought about for his fondness for "gluttling and gorging". Excess was something he could enjoy and for a man who stood some 6' 3" it would appear to the eye that, initially at least, his large frame could absorb much of that excess.

However, Thackeray's lazy attitude to completely mastering anything he set his mind too, especially where ambition for academia was involved, meant he departed Cambridge little more than a year after joining. He had however published two short works in University periodicals. As an author, he would have quite some impact on English literature in the years to come, so it seems difficult to reconcile that he felt no urgency to pursue writing at that time.

He now spent some time travelling across Europe stopping at both Paris, to study art, and to winter in Weimar. Back in London a final attempt was made on a professional career. This time studying law at Middle Temple. It lasted no more than a few months.

Now, having reached 21, he received his father's inheritance. It was a very substantial estate of 17,000 pounds, an enormous sum of money at the time. However, although Thackeray had youth he lacked a little in energy and certainly much financial experience. He funded not one but two newspapers, and neither was to prove successful. Gambling seemed enjoyable and certainly he had money to lose, which he did on a regular basis. Further investments in two soon-to-fail Indian banks quickly ensured little of his good fortune remained.

He now had to consider taking up yet another profession. Thackeray turned to art hoping that his studies in Paris would prove of benefit. Unfortunately, they did not. His ambivalent attitude continued until on August 20th, 1836 he married the 20-year-old, Isabella Gethin Shawe. It seemed to prove a turning point in many ways.

The marriage would produce three daughters; Anne Isabella in 1837, Jane, in 1838, who tragically died in infancy and Harriet Marian in 1840.

Now, as a husband and father, Thackeray seemed at last to understand his responsibilities to nurture and provide.

His early efforts at "writing for his life" were to establish his career as a foremost author. His main employment was with Fraser's Magazine, a sharp-witted and sharp-tongued conservative publication for which he produced art criticism, short fictional sketches, and who would also serialise two of his novels. He also found time, between 1837 and 1840 to review books for The Times and to make regular contributions to The Morning Chronicle and The Foreign Quarterly Review.

In his earliest works, which he wrote under various pseudonyms including; Charles James Yellowplush, Michael Angelo Titmarsh and George Savage Fitz-Boodle, he tended towards savagery in his attacks on high society, military prowess, the institution of marriage and hypocrisy.

Between May 1839 and February 1840 Fraser's published Catherine. Originally intended as a satire of the Newgate school of crime fiction, it ended up being more of a picaresque tale. Thackeray also began work on what would eventually become A Shabby Genteel Story.

However, Thackeray, having successfully found a career that he cared about and had the talent for, found that his personal life was about to descend into chaos. After the birth of her third child in 1840, Isabella, sank into depression. At first Thackeray, didn't think too much of it. He needed to work to earn an income to support his family and finding that Isabella was distracting both herself and him he realised he could get no work done at home and so spent more and more time away until finally, in September 1840, it dawned upon him how serious his wife's condition had become. Struck by guilt, he set out with his wife to Ireland. During the boat crossing she threw herself into the sea, but was thankfully pulled from the waters. Her mother who had little understanding of her daughter's illness was of little help and perhaps a hinderance. After four-weeks they returned to England. From November 1840 to February 1842 Isabella was in and out of professional care, as her condition waxed and waned.

Isabella eventually deteriorated into a permanent state of detachment. Thackeray desperately sought cures for her, but nothing worked, and she ended up in two different asylums in or near Paris until 1845, after which Thackeray took her back to England, where he installed her with a Mrs Bakewell at Camberwell. Despite her condition Isabella would outlive her husband by 3 decades.

After his wife's illness Thackeray became a de facto widower, never able to establish another permanent relationship.

In 1843, through his connection to the illustrator John Leech, whom he had met at Charterhouse, he began writing for the newly created magazine Punch, in which he published The Snob Papers, later collected as The Book of Snobs. Thackeray was a regular contributor to Punch until 1854.

Thackeray had earlier received some success with two travel books, The Paris Sketch Book and The Irish Sketch Book, the latter marked by hostility to Irish Catholics. The book appealed to British prejudices, and on that basis Thackeray now became Punch's Irish expert, often under the pseudonym Hibernis Hibernior. It was Thackeray's writings that were the basis for Punch's notoriously harsh, hostile and condescending depictions of the Irish during the devastating Irish Famine (1845–51).

As well as his regular columns and contributions Thackeray worked on his novels. In The Luck of Barry Lyndon, which was serialised in Fraser's in 1844, he explored the situation of an outsider trying to achieve status in high society, a theme he developed more successfully a few years later with Vanity Fair.

Thackeray achieved more recognition with his Snob Papers (serialised 1846/7, and published as a book in 1848), but the work that really established his fame was the novel Vanity Fair, which first appeared in serialised instalments beginning in January 1847.

Published as a book the novel had a slow start but eventually sales rose to 7,000 copies a month. Just as importantly, it was the book that everybody was talking about. Thackeray finally had a name that gained notice and was reviewed in journals such as the famed, and much sought after, Edinburgh Review.

The accolades and success also gave him a respite from writing everything in a manner that would help ensure income rather than literary respect. Even before Vanity Fair completed its serial run Thackeray had become a celebrity, sought after by the very lords and ladies whom he satirised. with the character of Becky Sharp, the artist's daughter who rises high by manipulating all around her.

Pendennis followed in 1849-50, but it was interrupted halfway through writing for 3 months by a severe illness. Some accounts say it was cholera. Pendennis is a semi-autobiographical bildungsroman that draws on, among other things, Thackeray's disappointments in college, his ambivalent relationship with his mother, and his insider's knowledge of the London publishing world.

This novel ran at the same time as Charles Dicken's David Copperfield, and their dual appearance brought about the first of many comparisons with Dickens. Thackeray, for his part, felt that he and

Dickens were battling for supremacy, though he would never equal Dickens's popularity, except with the critics.

Interestingly the two were involved in a spat which became known as the "Garrick Club affair". Thackeray and Dickens had skirmished over the "Dignity of Literature" and had other slight disagreements but this literary quarrel caused a rift in their friendship that lasted almost until the end of Thackeray's life. The relationship was healed only in Thackeray's last months, through a surprise meeting and handshake on the steps of a London club. Thackeray had taken offense at some personal remarks in a column by Edmund Yates and demanded an apology, eventually taking the affair to the Garrick Club committee. Already upset with Thackeray for an indiscreet remark about his affair with Ellen Ternan, Dickens championed Yates, helping him to write letters both to Thackeray and, in his defense, to the club's committee. Despite the intervention of Dickens, Yates eventually lost the vote of the Club's members, but the quarrel was laid out for the public in journal articles and pamphlets. "What pains me most," Thackeray said at the time, "is that Dickens should have been his adviser, and next that I should have had to lay a heavy hand on a young man who, I take it, has been cruelly punished by the issue of the affair, and I believe is hardly aware of the nature of his own offence, and doesn't even now understand that a gentleman should resent the monstrous insult which he volunteered".

Aside from these quarrelsome, distracting literary disagreements and Isabella's on-going illness life was good for Thackeray. He was to remain as he put it "at the top of the tree," for the rest of his life. The works for which he is so well remembered; Vanity Fair and Barry Lyndon had established that but he continued to write and produce novels, stories, sketches and works profusely.

To remain at such a high level in both quality and quantity is somewhat surprising given the continuation and escalation of various illnesses which continued to haunt him.

With Isabella still unwell Thackeray did seek out other women, in particular Mrs Jane Brookfield. Despite his hopes, it always felt that he was pursuing her as she battled the problems of her own marriage and turned to Thackeray for comfort and support. A source for these relationships often came on the lecture tours of Great Britain and the United States which he now entertained. These tours gave the public a chance to see and hear their hero's and provided another valuable source of income for those invited to tour. Whilst in in New York he met the Baxter family. Sally, the eldest daughter, enchanted the novelist—as a number of vibrant, intelligent, beautiful young women had done before her—and she became the model for Ethel Newcome. He visited her on his second tour of the States when she was married to a South Carolina gentleman. His choosing of married women in the shape of both Jane and Sally was ill-advised and both relationships led nowhere but did take quite some time to disassemble and for reason to set in.

In 1852, The History of Henry Esmond was published as a 3-volume novel without first being serialised and in a special type meant to imitate the appearance of an eighteenth-century book. This was the most carefully planned of Thackeray's novels. The book was celebrated for its brilliance, and Thackeray recognized it as "the very best I can do". At the time, it caused a sensation thanks to its controversial ending, wherein the hero marries a woman who early in the novel seemed more like a "mother" to him.

The eighteenth-century held a great attraction for Thackeray and he had previously set both Barry Lyndon and Catherine there as well as the sequel to Esmond, The Virginians, which takes place in North America and includes George Washington as a character.

Thackeray had twice visited the United States on lecture tours during this period as well as given lectures in London on the English humorists of the eighteenth century, and on the first four Hanoverian monarchs. The latter were published in a book as The Four Georges.

Interestingly Thackeray also decided that Politics was something he could more than dabble in. In Oxford he stood as an independent for Parliament. He was narrowly beaten by Cardwell, a politician who was substituted for the man Thackeray thought he was going to run against, although Thackeray's advocacy of entertainment on the Sabbath would have done little to help his campaign. Even so the margin of his defeat was only 1,070 votes, to Thackeray's 1,005.

In 1860 Thackeray became editor of the newly established Cornhill Magazine, a role he never felt truly comfortable in, preferring to contribute as a columnist on the Roundabout Papers. However, the financial compensation was by all accounts quite extraordinary. The Cornhill began its history with a record circulation and a number of distinguished contributors swayed onboard by Thackeray's reputation. It was in the Cornhill that he serialised his last complete novel, The Adventures of Philip in 1861-62. (After his death, the incomplete Denis Duval would also appear there in 1864).

After two years as editor he stepped down, primarily to concentrate on writing novels again. A piece he wrote for the Cornhill at this time "Thorns in the Cushion," one of The Roundabout Papers, fondly assembles the pains he felt in rejecting manuscripts on the one hand and receiving criticism of the magazine on the other. It seemed a good time to move on.

Thackeray's health had worsened during the 1850s and he was plagued by a recurring stricture of the urethra that laid him up for days at a time. He also felt that he had lost much of his creative impetus. He worsened matters by excessively eating and drinking, and avoiding exercise, though he enjoyed horseback-riding. He has been described as "the greatest literary glutton who ever lived". Indeed, his main activity apart from writing was eating and drinking and many of his stories include elaborate scenes and themes on his fondness for them.

On December 23rd, 1863, William Makepeace Thackeray, after returning from dining out and before dressing for bed, suffered a massive stroke. He was found dead on his bed the following morning. He was only fifty-two.

His death was entirely unexpected, and shocked family, friends and indeed the entire Nation.

It is said that at his funeral service thousands of mourners turned out to witness his passing. He was buried on December 29th at Kensal Green Cemetery, London.

William Makepeace Thackeray – A Concise Bibliography

The Yellowplush Papers (1837)
Catherine (1839–40)
A Shabby Genteel Story (1840)
Second Funeral of Napoleon (1841)
The Irish Sketchbook (1843)
The Luck of Barry Lyndon (1844)

Notes of a Journey from Cornhill to Grand Cairo (1846)
Mrs. Perkins's Ball (1846), under the name M. A. Titmarsh
Stray Papers: Being Stories, Reviews, Verses, and Sketches (1821-1847)
The Book of Snobs (1848)
Vanity Fair (1848)
Pendennis (1848–1850)
Rebecca and Rowena (1850)
The Paris Sketchbook (1840)
Men's Wives (1852)
The History of Henry Esmond (1852)
The English Humorists of the Eighteenth Century (1853)
The Newcomes (1855)
The Rose and the Ring (1855)
The Virginians (1857–1859)
Lovel the Widower (1860)
Four Georges (1860-1861)
The Adventures of Philip (1862)
Roundabout Papers (1863)
Denis Duval (1864)
The English Humorists of the eighteenth century: A Series of Six Lectures (1867)
Ballads (1869)
Burlesques (1869)
The Orphan of Pimlico (1876)

Thackeray wrote a numerous number of articles for magazines and the like as well as contributing many picture sketches to articles and his own books. Many were then collected and published together. We have listed his major works only for this bibliography.

www.ingramcontent.com/pod-product-compliance
Lightning Source LLC
Chambersburg PA
CBHW061456170626
46811CB00004B/1534